hokey pokey

Also by Jerry Spinelli

Stargirl

Love, Stargirl

Milkweed

Crash

Knots in My Yo-yo String:
The Autobiography of a Kid

with Eileen Spinelli

Today I Will

jerry spinelli
hokey pokey

A YEARLING BOOK

Text copyright © 2013 by Jerry Spinelli
Cover art copyright © 2013 by Shutterstock
Map copyright © 2013 by David Leonard

All rights reserved. Published in the United States by Yearling, an imprint of Random House Children's Books, a division of Random House LLC, a Penguin Random House Company, New York. Originally published in hardcover in the United States by Alfred A. Knopf, an imprint of Random House Children's Books, New York, in 2013.

Yearling and the jumping horse design are registered trademarks of Random House LLC.

Visit us on the Web! randomhouse.com/kids

Educators and librarians, for a variety of teaching tools, visit us at
RHTeachersLibrarians.com

The Library of Congress has cataloged the hardcover edition of this work as follows:
Spinelli, Jerry.
Hokey Pokey / by Jerry Spinelli. — 1st ed.
p. cm.
Summary: Ever since they were Snotsippers, Jack and the girl have fought, until one day she steals his bike, and as he and the Amigos try to recover it, Jack realizes that he is growing up and must eventually leave the "goodlands and badlands of Hokey Pokey."
ISBN 978-0-375-83198-0 (trade) — ISBN 978-0-375-93198-7 (lib. bdg.) —
ISBN 978-0-375-83201-7 (tr. pbk.) — ISBN 978-0-307-97570-6 (ebook)
[1. Play—Fiction. 2. Growth—Fiction.] I. Title.
PZ7.S75663Ho 2013 [Fic]—dc23 2012004177

ISBN 978-0-440-42051-4 (pbk.)

Printed in the United States of America
10 9 8 7 6 5 4 3 2 1
First Yearling Edition 2014

Random House Children's Books supports the First Amendment
and celebrates the right to read.

To Norristown

"Daddy, what does tomorrow mean?"
—Madison Stokes, age 4
Hershey, Pennsylvania
November 22, 2008

"Kids. They live in their own little world."
—Jack's father
Saturday morning

WHAT IS HOKEY POKEY?

A place

A time

A square snowball treat

A circle dance

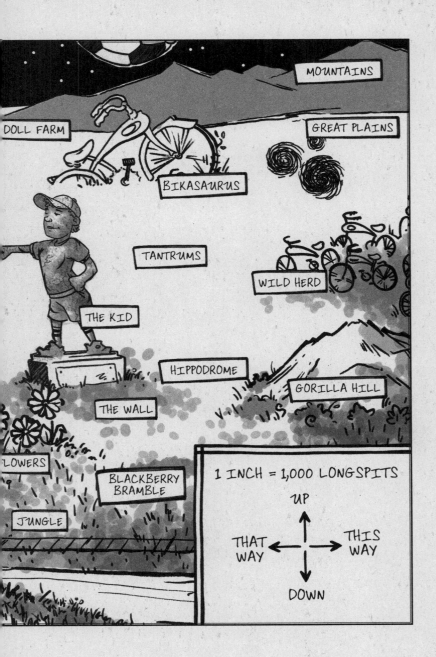

NIGHT

ALL NIGHT LONG Seven Sisters whisper and giggle and then, all together, they rush Orion the Hunter and tickle him, and Orion the Hunter laughs so hard he shakes every star in the sky, not to mention Mooncow, who loses her balance and falls—*puh-loop!*—into Big Dipper, which tip-tip-tips and dumps Mooncow into Milky Way, and Mooncow laughs and splashes and rolls on her back and goes floating down down down Milky Way, and she laughs a great moomoonlaugh and kicks at a lavender star and the star goes shooting across the sky, up the sky and down the sky, a lavender snowfireball down the highnight down . . .

down . . .

down . . .

down . . .

TODAY

JACK

. . . TO HOKEY POKEY . . .

    . . . where it lands, a golden bubble now, a starborn bead, lands and softly pips upon the nose of sleeping Jack and spills a whispered word:
    it's
and then another:
time

◆

Something is wrong.
He knows it before he opens his eyes.
He looks.

His bike is gone!

Scramjet!

What more could he have done? He parked it so close that when he shut his eyes to sleep, he could smell the rubber of the tires, the grease on the chain.

And still she took it. His beloved Scramjet. He won't say her name. He never says her name, only her kind, sneers it to the morning star: *"Girl."*

He runs to the rim of the bluff, looks up the tracks, down the tracks. There she is, ponytail flying from the back of her baseball cap, the spokes of the wheels—*his* wheels—plumspun in the thistledown dawn.

He waves his fist, shouts from the bluff: "I'll get you!"

The tracks curve, double back. He can cut her off!

He sneakerskis down the gullied red-clay slope, leaps the tracks, plunges into the jungle and runs—*phloot!*—into a soft, vast, pillowy mass. *Oh no! Not again!* He only thinks this. He cannot say it because the front half of himself, including his face, is buried in the hippopotamoid belly of Wanda's monster. This has happened before. He wags his head hard, throws it back, and—*ttthok!*—his face comes free.

"Wan-daaa!" he bellows. "Wake up!"

Wanda stirs in a bed of mayapples.

"Wanda!"

The moment Wanda awakes, her monster vanishes in a puff of apricots, dropflopping Jack to the ground. He's up in an instant and off again.

Every other step is a leap over a sleeper. All is quiet save thunder beyond the trees and the thump of the sun bumping the underside of the horizon.

He hoprocks across the creek, past the island of Forbidden Hut, and pulls up huffing at the far loop end of the tracks. He looks up, looks down.

Nothing.

He slumps exhausted to the steel rail. He stares at his sneaker tops. He gasps, reflects. She said she would do it. "I'm going to take—" No, to be accurate, she didn't say *take*, she said *ride:* "I'm going to ride your bike." And who knows? Maybe if she had said it nicely . . . maybe if she wasn't a girl. But she *is* a girl and she said it with that snaily smirk, but there was no way she was ever coming within ten long spits of his bike.

But she did.

And he hates her. He hates her for taking the thing he loves most in this world. But maybe even more, he hates her for being right.

He pushes himself up from the rail. Once more he casts forlorn eyes up and down the tracks that no train travels. He cries out: "Scramjet!" This is too painful to bear alone. From the black tarpit of despair he rips his Tarzan yell and hurls it into the jungle and over the creek and across the dreamlands of Hokey Pokey.

A SMALL BROWN BIRD

Flies over the Mountains, spreads its tiny wings high above Hokey Pokey and rides the riptide of Jack's despair.

Over Flowers and The Wall and the mutter of bad-words in Jailhouse sails the call of Tarzan. Over Snuggle Stop and Tattooer and Tantrums and Stuff. Veering wide around Socks, over Thousand Puddles and Doll Farm and Trucks. Over Great Plains and the wild herd flies Jack's lament, over sleepers sleeping and monsters monstering and all the badlands and goodlands of Hokey Pokey to the ever-listening ears of Jack's best pals: LaJo and Dusty. Amigos.

Dusty has slept in his favorite spot, under the out-stretched, monumental arm of The Kid. LaJo—who, like most Hokey Pokers, sleeps where he drops—has bunked in Flowers. Both hear at the same moment. Both hear more than the usual morning call. Both hear: *Pain!* Both hear: *Help!* Up from the ground, into the saddles, homing in on the sound waves: *Tracks . . . farside bend.* Pounding pedals, gravel flying, together returning the yodeling call: *Coming!*

DESTROYER

IF YOU WANT TO GO LONG, you can call him Most Amazing Terrible Ever Destroyer of Worlds. If you want to go short, call him Destroyer. But don't call *him* short. And don't call him Harold Peter Bitterman Jr.

It is the return Tarzan call that awakens Destroyer. He has spent the night, as always, high in the remote-controlled SuperScoop of his cherry-red eight-wheeled Mark X BullDogger dump truck, Hokey Pokey's biggest toy. He lazes on his back. The high, thin clouds look like truck exhaust tinged with pink. A brown bird flies overhead. He wishes he had a stone. He catches a whiff of apricots—and jerks fully awake, sits up. This is the day! He hopes he's not too late. He peers over the edge of his high hoist. His kingdom sprawls below him. He spots a dustball rolling across Great Plains. Here and there a monster dissolves in a pale yellow puff, but most are still there, hovering over their dopey little sleepers.

He's got to move fast. He grabs the remote, punches DOWN. With a click and jerk, the great red cradle stirs, swings, lowers him slowly to the ground. He punches the remote—SuperScoop returns to its up spot. He dashes around to the cab, jumps in, plants his feet on the pedals—Wait! Clothespin! . . . Does he have it? He feels into his pocket. . . . Yes, OK, move! He pushes—right foot, left foot, churns, churns. . . . Bull-Dogger lumbers off.

AMIGOS

Two sides of an arrowhead, two bikes, come to a
point at Jack, slumpsitting on the rusty rail. LaJo, Dusty
glance about.

"Where's—" says Dusty.

"—Scramjet?" says LaJo.

"She stole it," says Jack. He doesn't have to say who
she is.

"Glove too?" says LaJo.

Jack hasn't even thought of his baseball glove,
looped over the handlebar of the bike. Where he goes,
the glove goes. He nods heavily.

They cannot speak. They do not know Jack without his bike. Things have shifted.

They dismount.

Jack pulls up his shirt and pretends to wipe sweat from his face, but really, even though he wants them here, he doesn't want to be seen.

LaJo stares in shock, is about to say something, clears his throat, says something else: "You crying?"

Jack springs, shoves LaJo backward. LaJo's bike clatters to the ground. "Do I *look* like I'm crying? Did you *ever* catch me crying?"

Jack kicks LaJo's bike tire, glares, dares him to do something about it. He turns to Dusty. "Did *you?*"

Dusty flashes a V-finger peace sign. "Hey, not that I ever saw."

Jack is in his face. "Not that *you* ever saw? What's that mean? *You* never saw me but somebody else *did?*" Poking him in the chest. "Huh?"

"No, man." Dusty puts up his hands as if sheriff-caught. "I ain't sayin that. You never . . . you just ain't a crier, Jackarooni—everybody knows that."

Jack gives Dusty's bike a kick and scuffs down the tracks, stops, sags, shows them his back.

Dusty calls: "Scramjet. He was a great one, Amigo. Right, LJ?"

"Yeah," says LaJo.

Jack is silent, still. Then says something they cannot hear.

Both call, "What?"

Jack wheels. "What do you mean *was*?"

LaJo straddles his fallen bike. "Hey, man—"

Dusty rushes forward, laughing too loud. "*Sí, sí,* Amigo! What's this *was* stuff? We just got to get it back, is all." He punches Jack's arm. He gives a sneery laugh. "Ain't no *was*." He spits in the dirt, gives Jack another punch.

Jack returns the punch. A grin peeks over the edge of his scowl. "I know where she'll head," he says.

Dusty yips like a puppy. "Yeah! Where?"

Jack pulls LaJo's bike to its feet. He mounts the rear fender. He looks from one to the other. "Gorilla Hill," he says. And in their eyes and growing grins he sees the truth of it.

GORILLA HILL

Two bikes, three Amigos crunch the cinders back along the looping rails to the off-track side of the bluff: Gorilla Hill. They stow the bikes in the brush at the foot. "Hurry," says Jack. They lean into the hard, yellow, mica-flecked trail. It's downhill heaven but uphill hell. The sweat and the sun on LaJo's brown skin give his forehead the sparkle of a root beer hokey pokey. Jack's hatred grows with every step, every thigh-crunching reminder of his shame—this epic, this magnificent hill is for riding down, not walking up.

Suddenly up ahead, beyond the bow-bend, up, out of the glittering sky itself, a voice: "Yee-hah!"

Dusty cries, "She's coming!"

"Off the trail!" barks LaJo.

They cannot see yet but they can hear: the chittering chain and axles, the stone-pocked crunch of rubber, the thief's crazed scream unfurling. They can feel the speed, feel it accelerate with every wheelturn, feel the hill snuffle and grin and stiffen its spine, feel the air split like a snapped stick as into the bow-bend they lean.

"Yeeeeeeeeeeeeeeeeeeee—"

"Now!" cries Dusty.

"Holy crap!" cries LaJo.

And out of the bow-bend they come as the sun at last thrusts its bristling fist into the sky and blinds the boys to all but the high sonic scream of chainsong and a hissing shadowblur of steed and she-demon blasting out of the sunfire.

"HAAAAAAAAAAAH!"

"Scraaaaaamjet!" Jack cries, but his voice is already a hole in the afterwind.

In time the Amigos stagger onto the trail, blinking, shading their eyes. Already bike and rider are a flying speck halfway to Great Plains. They appear to be one. Stunned, silent, the boys begin their grim descent. They avoid each other's eyes. Beneath their sneaker soles the trail is warm. The air smells of girl and burnt rubber.

JUBILEE

Jubilates!

Churns—no hands!—across Great Plains, whooping, laughing, scattering the wild herd of bikes in a fright of dust and spitting stones. The thrill, the exhilaration of the downhill dive—the freefall of it, the uncontrol, the *flight*!—she has never known before.

The handlebar dips, veers to the left: feeling the pull of the old herd. Oh yes, she thinks, how wonderful to be wild again, racing dust devils across the Plains. Should she let the beast go, rejoin the herd? Should she? . . . No! Maybe someday but not now, not yet. Now there is only the thrill! The power! The speed!

And no more *Scramjet*. No more *he*. "No!" she shouts full voice over the flatlands. She jacks her elbows, leans forward till the tire spins inches below her face, the prairie a weedy blur. "Hazel," she whispers. "You are"—she straightens, shouts—"Haaazzzzzz-el!"

She giggles at her own brilliance. She knows the name Hazel is dumb, but her opinion doesn't matter. What matters is *his* opinion, the boy's. The germ's. When he hears what she's renamed his pride and joy— oh she wishes she could be there to see it!

She shouts: "Hazel! Hazel! Hazel!" She wishes there was somebody to celebrate with, to high-five, but there is only herself and Hazel and the wild wheeled mustangs. So she gives Hazel her head and high-fives— high-tens!—the morning sky.

DESTROYER

GREAT!

The kid is still sleeping, his monster bobbing above him. Ugliest monster Destroyer has ever seen. Which figures: the wimpier the kid, the grosser the monster. Days of scouting have led to this moment. The victim has been carefully chosen. He has three things going for him:

1. He's tiny. Of course, he's a Newbie.

2. He's weak and wimpy. Of course, he's a Newbie.

3. He sleeps on the ground. He's a Cartoons freak. Every night he flops in the same spot practically inches

from the enormous screen. The scoop-up will be a piece of cake.

Destroyer steers around the many bodies that litter the massive lawn. Cartoons never stop on the big screen. *The Flintstones* is showing now. This is where he first saw Daffy Duck. This is the first time he's been back here since The Worst Thing That Ever Happened happened. The memory makes him want to cry. But he doesn't.

He pulls up to the victim, stops. He punches the remote. Down comes SuperScoop, flush to the ground. Gently, toes on pedals, he inches the scoop forward till he feels resistance—the kid's body. He stops. The kid's monster, a watermelon-headed joker with green fangs the size of bananas, floats in the dawn like a balloon, looks brainlessly down on Destroyer. This is the tricky part. Destroyer readies his feet, takes a deep breath— *now!* The scoop slides forward, under the kid. Destroyer punches UP, then REVERSE. SuperScoop thrusts skyward. BullDogger rumbles. The kid wakens and wails. The monster vanishes in an apricotty mist. Destroyer churns.

Past Trucks, on toward a gray hill that rises from a desert barren of even weed and insect. Destroyer stops at the edge of the desert. The red cradle is rocking on high, the Newbie is shrieking, going nutso. "Hold yer pants on!" Destroyer calls, and laughs. He digs the clothespin from his pocket, clips it onto his nose, honks "Hold yer smeller!" and churns onward. Closer, the hill resolves itself into shades and scraps of gray . . . into . . . Socks. It is a heap, a mountain of dirty socks so disgusting that life in all its forms steers clear. In the red cradle the Newbie victim gets his first whiff, and now the red cradle rocks and lurches to the peals of terror from the doomed Newbie.

Breathing through his mouth, Destroyer churns on. The air itself becomes gray, mossy. Destroyer doesn't bring BullDogger to a halt until the front tires are noogling into the flank of the monstrous heap. He wishes he'd brought cotton for his ears; the screams are deafening. He lowers SuperScoop till it sways a mere body length above the gray slope, which close up seems to be roiling from the power of the stench. He reaches for the remote. He punches FLIP. The red cradle abruptly turns upside down. Into the unholy heap falls the Newbie.

Destroyer backchurns, turns and pedals off as fast as his legs will go. He discovers it's almost impossible to pedal hard and laugh hard at the same time.

JACK

THREE AMIGOS LEAVE TWO BIKES in the brush at the foot of the hill. If one can't ride, nobody rides. Sunlight is sour on the tongue.

Squinting in the yellow dust, Jack says, "Let's split up. Cover more territory that way."

"Rippin," says Dusty.

"What do we do if just one of us finds her?" says LaJo.

"How many you need to stop a girl?" says Jack.

"Yeah, LJ," says Dusty, grinning. "Want me to come with you? 'Case you need help, Amigo?"

Jack pokes them both. "Just do it. I don't care how. Just get the bike back."

They start off in three directions. LaJo mutters something.

Jack stops. "What?"

"He said *on foot*," says Dusty, swallowing a giggle.

Jack stares. "OK, fine. LaJo, just stay here. Go lie down there in the weeds and kiss your bike."

LaJo sniffs. "No."

"No? What no?"

"No, you ain't my boss. None of us is boss. We're equal."

Jack and LaJo commence a stare-down, neither knowing what to say next. After a while LaJo's eyes drift to the side, causing Jack to turn. Dusty is standing square at the foot of the hill, looking up.

"What're *you* looking at?" says Jack.

Dusty doesn't appear to have heard the question. His eyes are slits in the sun but he doesn't shade them. His voice is dreamy. "She came down that hill—" They wait for more but that's all, until he says it again, this time with a touch of wonder on the word *down:* "She came *down* that hill—"

Jack opens his mouth but says nothing. He gives up.

What's the use? He spits in the dust. "Good." He walks off. But feels LaJo's stare. Stops. Turns. LaJo is not just looking. He's not just staring. He's staring funny. Strange. Jack shows his disgust with a blow of breath. "*Now* what?"

LaJo shrugs, blank-eyed. "Nothin."

"I'll stand here all day, man."

Another shrug. "You're different. That's all."

"Different?"

"Yeah."

"Different how?"

A third shrug. Unlike normal people, LaJo prefers to communicate with his shoulders.

Jack turns to Dusty. "I look *different* to you?"

"Lemme see." Dusty curls his hands into tubes, stacks them and peers through the telescope. "Yes . . . yes . . . I think I see . . ."

Jack is taken aback. For a second he half believes his goofy pal is actually detecting something. "What?"

Dusty continues to study, nodding. "Yes . . . yes . . ."

"*What?*"

Dusty looks up. His face is serious. He speaks: "Your bike . . . is"—he peers down the tube a final time—"gone."

Jack blinks. If he doesn't leave this instant, he'll kill

them both. He turns and heads off. And hears . . . something . . . something far away . . . a sound he's never heard before and yet he somehow knows. He thinks to turn, ask them if they hear it, but they're busy yukking at Dusty's big joke.

He doesn't look back. He knows they're already heading off in other directions. He's in too bad a mood to say it out loud, but he knows, in their own bumbling ways, they'll try.

He walks. It feels weird—walking. He can't remember the last time he did it. Running, yes—baseball, football, races, horsing around—always running. But starting the day he mounted his first nag, he's never walked anywhere longer than back-to-back spits.

He's forgotten how slowly the world inches along when you're walking. He's forgotten that walking, specifically walking by yourself, leads to thinking. He remembers the day Scramjet came into his life. . . .

The three of them—himself, Dusty, LaJo—were idly cruising Great Plains when the wild herd went thundering by. The Amigos pulled up to witness the awesome spectacle, unconscious grins on their faces. The magnificence, the unbridled wildness! The dust plume they raised shone golden in the sun, as if a celestial cloud had just then set them down from their home in some paradise of gods.

But what got Jack's attention most on that hot and steamy day—iced him as surely as if a slushy hokey pokey had been dropped down his shirt—was the sight of the leader, a stallion the likes of which he had never seen in all his days, a black-and-silver beauty who led his mustangs as regally as any emperor.

The Amigos sometimes amused themselves by chasing down and roping an old grandpa straggler, then releasing him with a laugh. Stories of prime mounts taken from the wild herd were legendary—and rare. Most kids rode hand-me-downs. Jack's wasn't even that. It was a bent, wobbly-wheeled misfit he should have scrapped long ago.

He dismounted. He grabbed his junker by the handlebar post and mangy saddle and hurled it across the parched land. He shoved Dusty from his nag, climbed aboard and took off after the golden cloud. For in those brief seconds he had for the first time seen both his own miserable condition and his glorious future.

Normally it was phantoms, or maybe history, the wild herd fled from, and the flights, though many, were brief, as these things come and go. But this was something else, this was a boy riding not just a bike but a mission, and what he lacked in speed he made up for in got-to. It wasn't long into the chase before the cloud broke into spatters as all but the leader peeled away, and it came to Jack sharp and solid as a bat fat on a fastball that the herd was quite unaccidentally leaving the field to the two of them and their shared destiny.

Jack bore down. Sweat popped from his eyelashes. His cap was long gone. All his fire funneled down to the balls of his feet, which he had to mightily concentrate on or they'd go flying off the pedals.

Across the crackling Plains they raced, the stallion a home-run poke ahead, when all of a sudden it slowed down. Slowed down and stopped. *And turned!* Turned to face its pursuer.

Jack pulled up—shocked, puzzled. He looked behind, looked around, saw nothing but Great Plains, nothing but dust and smears of wild rye and tumbleweed. Dead ahead stood the great beast, perfectly still, at once magnificent and terrible, emitting a faint, silvery radiance that Jack swore he could hear. The tires, where the rubber met the dust, were faintly heaving. Steam rose from the black leather saddle. Somewhere a coyote howled.

Every atom of the steed was aimed at Jack. Was it

going to charge? The stallion was now moving again, moving forward, slowly, unmistakably, right for him. He foot-pushed Dusty's bike backward. He turned the front wheel to two o'clock. He pressed one foot down, ready on the high-side pedal . . .

And on that morning of surprises, experienced another: fear did not come. Feeling unright, he reached for fear, but it was not there. He blinked. Onward came the stallion—he could now hear the tires' groundcrinkle—yet stare as he dared, he found no menace. In goggle-eyed, gape-mouthed shock he stood there like a dummy as the steed advanced until in all its imperial presence it stood no more than two feet in front of him. And somewhere in his mortal brain a miraculous thought unfolded like the morning wings of a dragonfly: *I have been blessed.* Something in his undeserving, unremarkable boyself had apparently caught the eye of the King of the Plains, and the King was doing no less than conferring on him a kind of knighthood of equals.

Well (Jack smiles to recall), with a small condition—for as he shed Dusty's nag and curled his trembling fingers around the steed's regal, ribbed handlegrips, as he solemnly placed his left foot in the left stirrup, as he brazenly swung his right leg over and settled into the sunwarmed saddle, the King rose up on its hind wheel, pawed at the clouds and proceeded to give him the fright and the thrill of his lifetime. Thinking back on it later, Jack decided that it would have been an insult to the Law of the Plains for any great wild one to submit without a fight, even to an equal. A steed must be himself. A rider must prove himself.

But for the moment there was no thinking, only hanging on for dear life as the stallion bucked and pitched and snapped and lurched in untamed fury to unseat its sitter. Most of the time the only parts of Jack in touch with the careening bronc were his hands, as his feet, legs and butt went flouncing in the air. But somehow he hung on, and finally, finally the steed slowed to a trot and—just like that—was no longer wild.

Was his.

AMIGOS

Dusty and LaJo have started out in different directions but now find themselves dovetailing back to each other. "Maybe we should separate," says Dusty. He looks at LaJo but gets no answer. "Jack said."

"So?"

Dusty pokes him. "You know what?" No answer. Pokes him again. "Man. Don't you even want to know *what*?"

LaJo's eyes are on his sneaker tips, kicking dirtballs. "What?"

"I'll tell you what. You always say *so*."

"So?"

Dusty cracks up. "See?" Pokes. "So. I'm gonna call you So Man." Still walking, he puts his face directly into LaJo's, sees the faint lipcurl. "See. You wanna say it again, don't ya? You're ready to say it again. . . . So."

LaJo grins—he can't help it. "So what do you think's gonna happen if we find her, you all that big talk back there."

"I don't know," says Dusty. "Lasso her."

"Yeah." LaJo smirks. "Right."

Dusty kicks dirtballs. "I'm just saying . . . I don't know . . . I just feel bad, is all. It's one thing to lose your bike, or to crack it up, but for somebody to steal it . . . man. And of all bikes, that one. And a girl did it. That girl!"

"Ain't just him," says LaJo. "It's costing us too. Look"—he takes two running steps and kicks a stone—"we're walking, ain't we?"

Dusty nods vigorously. "You got that right. I hate it." Looks at his feet. "Can't believe I'm doing it. All I'm saying is I feel bad. It could happen to any of us."

"Yeah." LaJo shoves him sideways. "Would you feel bad if it was my bike she stole?"

Dusty shoves back. "Hey, you know it, LJ. We're

Amigos." He holds his fist out for a bump. LaJo gives it a weak pat. A posse of Snotsippers crosses their path. They're pedaling trikes furiously, chasing a rider in front of them, jabbing, firing cap pistols, some shouting along with the cap-pop: *"Pow! Pow! Pow!"*

Dusty lunges, holds the last kid by the trike seat. "Hey, you seen Jack's bike around? Scramjet? It was stole by that girl. Jubilee. Huh?"

The Snotsipper tries to pedal but goes nowhere. He tries to smack Dusty's hand away. "Hey," he whines, "lemme go!" His arms are flailing.

"Let him go," says LaJo.

Dusty lets him go.

They walk some more.

LaJo scans the horizon. "You talk too much."

Dusty stops, shocked. "Huh? What's that s'pose to mean?"

LaJo shrugs. "What it says."

Dusty stays behind, talks louder as LaJo continues to walk. "Where'd *that* come from? What's *that* got to do with anything? Huh?" Louder. *"Huh?"*

All he sees is LaJo's back, LaJo's shrug. And now he's glad LaJo isn't turning, because he's feeling his eyes sting, his lip quiver. He snatches at a blue chicory flower, chews it, chews away the tears, the quiver, tells himself LaJo doesn't know, Jack doesn't know, nobody knows that he still cries—of all the Big Kids in Hokey Pokey, him, still.

He trots to catch up, says with a blithe, sobless flip, "Hey. I almost forgot. What did you mean back there— *he's different?*"

LaJo shrugs, looks ahead, thankfully doesn't check his face for tear tracks. "Just that. He's different."

"OK," Dusty persists, "but how? *How's* he different?"

LaJo rolls his eyes. He's tempted to say it again— *You talk too much*—get that chin quivering, but a Newbie, littlest of the little, bolts from nearby Tattooer screaming, "I'm a kid!" The Newbie trips over his own feet, belly flops, picks himself up, lurches suddenly sideways and runs smack into LaJo's legs. LaJo, fright on his face, backs up, but it's too late. The tiny galoot is already yanking up his shirt and showing off to LaJo his brand-new, barely dry tattoo. His skin is chalk-white. His hair is the color of a cherry hokey pokey. He yips it again: "I'm a kid!"

LaJo stares down, freezes.

Dusty laughs a whopper. This is LaJo's nightmare come true. When a first-day Newbie pops out of

Tattooer, he goes to the first Big Kid he sees and shows off his tattoo. It's instinct for the Newbie—duty for the Big Kid. It's his job to spend the first day with the Newbie, get him squared away, tell him what he needs to know about life on Hokey Pokey. Dusty has done it many times. He hangs around Tattooer just for the chance. Not LaJo. LaJo isn't good with little kids. He's always managed to avoid first-day Newbies. Until now.

Dusty stops laughing long enough to call, "Go, big bro!"

The Newbie looks straight up into LaJo's stern eyes. He says it again: "I'm a kid!"

"Congratulations," LaJo replies dryly.

It tickles Dusty to see the Newbie take LaJo's hand—finger, actually. The tiny white hand curls around the giant brown finger. "My name is William!" the Newbie chirps. "What's yours?"

LaJo doesn't answer.

LAJO

CANNOT BELIEVE this is happening. How did he get stuck with this runt? What was he doing anywhere near Tattooer anyway? He's losing it. He's off his game. And he knows why. It's Jack. But not what Dusty thinks. Dusty can't see farther than the snot at the end of his nose. It's not the stolen-bike-and-girl thing. It's something else. Something he saw back at the tracks. But what he saw wasn't the thing itself. What he saw was like a rustle in the bushes, a hint of something. He doesn't know what it is. He doesn't understand it. He can't see it. He doesn't *want* to see it. He only knows this: it's bad. Way worse than a stolen bike. Way, *way* worse.

William the runt keeps pulling LaJo's finger. "What's *your* name?" the runt whines. "What's *your* name? What's *your* name?"

"LaJo!" he yells, and yanks his finger away. The runt staggers backward, falls on his butt as if hit by a gust of wind. The runt is getting ready to cry but sees LaJo is laughing—LaJo can't help it—so the runt joins in. He pops up. He starts skipping along, pulling the big finger, piping to the world: "LaJo! . . . LaJo! . . ."

The runt points. "LaJo—what's that?"

"Cartoons."

"What's Cartoons?"

"Pictures."

"What's—"

"Don't ask." Up on the big screen Road Runner is chasing Wile E. Coyote. By law LaJo is supposed to stay with the runt the whole first day. And do everything the runt wants. But who's going to know if he sneaks off while the runt is staring gaga at some cartoon? "Why don't you stay here and see for yourself," he says to the runt.

The runt thinks about it for two seconds. "No!" he blurts, and lurches off, dragging LaJo.

It's LaJo's ordinary world but it's all new to the runt. "What's that? . . . What's that? . . ." It's not enough just to see. The runt has to touch everything, try everything.

Trucks. "You can drive them." The runt does, his tiny legs churning pedals. Garbage truck. Semi. Tanker.

Doll Farm. "For girls," LaJo says, but the runt goes and digs up his own anyway.

Tantrums. "It's where you go bananas," LaJo tells him.

"What's bananas?" says the runt.

Hippodrome. The runt makes LaJo join him in the mouth of the green hippo. Then the pink one.

Snuggle Stop. LaJo waits outside while the runt goes in. When the runt comes out, he shocks LaJo, cuddles LaJo's leg. LaJo shakes him off.

Jailhouse. Thousand Puddles. Playground.

LaJo is getting desperate. Every step along the grand tour of Hokey Pokey, he's on the lookout for a chance to ditch the runt. And finally it happens. Halfway between the DON'T sign and The Wall he spots a herd of puppies—followed, as always, by a herd of Newbies. "Look," he says, stuffing excitement into his voice, "*puppies!*"

The runt is already taking off when LaJo remembers

the Four Nevers. He has to give them to the runt. It's the law. He grabs the runt. "Wait."

The runt wails, "Puppies!"

"Just a sec. I gotta tell you something." With the runt squirming in his hands, LaJo recites: "Never pass a puddle without stomping it. Never go to sleep until the last minute. Never go near Forbidden Hut. Never kiss a girl. OK, go."

William the runt runs screaming after the puppies.

LaJo scuffs dust, walks. He sees something in the distance, on Great Plains. He shades his eyes. It's a dustpuff, rolling across the shimmering vastness. Too small to be the mustang herd. And now he hears it, a mere speck of sound riding the morning breeze off the Mountains. His boy's ear identifies it instantly: *Girl . . . whoop . . . happy.*

JUBILEE

Rides!

DESTROYER

IF EVERYBODY WASN'T ALREADY AWAKE, they sure are now thanks to the racket from the kid in Socks. The kid is heaving and screaming, "Help! Help!" as if he's drowning. All the dumbo has to do is stay calm, hold his nose and roll himself down the slope and onto flat land. But of course he's too panicked to think of that. He is, after all, just a Newbie.

Destroyer removes the clothespin from his nose, takes a sniff test. He's a good five frog flings away and still the reek is strong. He replaces the clothespin. He climbs out of the cab and sits on the roof. Good place to enjoy the show.

Little kids are coming from all directions, attracted by the racket. None get any closer than Destroyer. They're holding their noses, turning blue some of them. "Don't go no closer!" a voice honks. Other voices call: "Hang on, Henry!" "Breathe through yer mouth, Henry!"

What impresses Destroyer is this: so many. So many kids come running. Newbies and Snotsippers and Sillynillies and Gappergums. They're forming a giant circle around Socks. Around Henry. Where were they when the Big Kids came for Destroyer? Back when he was Harold. Back when it was him and Daffy and the heck with the rest of the world. How he loved that thing! It was the only toy he needed. The pedals were webbed feet, just like a duck's. The back scooped out like a ducktail. But the best part was the front fender, which was Daffy's duckbill. It not only looked like Daffy's bill, it *acted* like Daffy's bill. Whenever he mashed the big soft red button, the bill flapped open and out came a sound—"*Yaak! Yaak!*"—that was pure Daffy. The whole thing was yellow. Didn't bother Harold that the color was not black like the real Daffy. As far as he was concerned, he was aboard the real Daffy—"*Yaak! Yaak!*"—not a tricycle.

They came out of nowhere. One moment he was

riding happily through Thousand Puddles and next thing he knew there were cries of "Runt!" and he was hanging upside down. Somebody had him by the ankles. He was looking at three pairs of ratty Big Kid sneakers and hearing a hurricane of laughter. One of them somehow squeezed himself onto Daffy, knees out like wings. One pedal turn and the trike broke with a sickening snap.

This made them laugh even harder. He was passed from hands to hands, swung like he was a swing, his pocket treasures raining to the ground. They dunked him headfirst into one of the puddles and headed off, staggering. They were no longer laughing. They were gasping, "Oh man..." and "Oh wow..." As he crawled out of the water, he wondered what it must be like to be so totally happy that you use up all your laughter. Then he cried.

A kid, a trike: broken, both. And nobody came. Nobody came running. No mob of kids calling to *him*, bucking *him* up: *Hang in there, Harold!*

46

JACK

LITTLE KIDS ARE RUNNING. He hears a distant yowl, in the direction of Socks. Probably another unlucky runt tossed into the smelly pile. It happens. But it's the commotion within that occupies Jack. That banshee scream—"*Yeeeeeee-HAAAAAAAAH!*"—of the devil girl. His heart an empty bike rack. The wind wailing through the blown-open hole in his soul. LaJo's remark, which he can't shake: *You're different.* And here's the thing: he sensed it long before LaJo said it. He feels it now, scuffing across Great Plains. Is it an absence? A presence? Good? Bad? He can't tell. There are no words for it. Except . . . *different*. He has sensed it from the moment he woke up, from the foggy moment *before* he woke up and knew his bike was gone, from the moment he heard the strange whispered words, coming back to him now, rising from dust on his sneaks: *it's . . . time*

Kidcalls knock him into the present:

"Yo, Jack! Where's yer bike?"

"Hey, Jack! What happened?"

Big Kids are speedbiking through the Plains like unleashed dogs. He prays none of them see her on Scramjet. He doesn't think he could survive the embarrassment.

"Hey, Jack!"

"Hey, Jack!"

He wishes he were less popular, less visible.

Suddenly he's in a cross fire. There's always a war going on somewhere on Hokey Pokey. Dismounted Snotsippers crouch behind trikes, firing away at each other as if he's not there, cap pistols spitting red ribbons:

"*Pow!*"

"*Pow!*"

"*Pow!*"

"*Pow!*"

"*Pow!*"

Now they look up from their gunsights.

"Hey, Jack! C'mon—join the war!"

"Be on our side, Jack!"

"*Our* side!"

He pistol-points at them, goes "*Pow!*"—and half a dozen fall dead. One kid is giving it the old leg twitch. Another's got his tongue drooping out. Snotsippers love to play dead. Jack ought to know. He was one of the best. He used to practice. His specialty was the wide-eyed blinkless stare. Sipping breaths to keep his chest still. Other goners looked like they were sleeping, but Jack—Jack was *dead*. And once—so famously they still talk about it—he stayed dead for *hours*, even through the arrival and departure of the Hokey Pokey Man.

He walks on through the sweet, peppery cloud of cap powder.

"Hey, Jack! Hey, Jack!"

Kiki comes running. He's waving something—Jack's baseball glove. The devil girl must have flung it from the handlebar. Kiki is gasping.

"Jack . . . Jack . . . look . . . Ifound . . . yourglove."

Jack takes it, holds it by the thumb, shakes it. A

desert of dust pours from the fingers. He wants to cry. He spits on the humped, leathery heel. As he wipes the dust away, the signature in silvery handwriting comes back into view: MR. SHORTSTOP.

Kiki gulps air, stares up at him in wide-eyed bafflement. "I found it out there"—he points—"on the ground. I knew it was yours. What"—he glances about—"where's your bike? Where's Scramjet? Huh, Jack? Dusty riding it? LaJo? Huh?"

Jack turns his back on Kiki's babble, walks.

"Jack, hey, look—I taped up my ball." He pounds it into his own glove, a cheap, thin imitation. Kiki's laces are plastic; Jack's are prime rawhide. "C'mon, Jack, throw me a coupla grounders, OK? Just a couple, huh, Jack?"

The black-taped ball comes rolling alongside, passes him as if it's going his way. It stops in the yellow dust ahead. "C'mon, Jack! C'mon!" Jack hears the slap of Kiki's fist in cheap leather. When he reaches the ball, he kicks it as hard as he can. It skitters across the prairie, coming to rest in a gray tangle of tumbleweed. The silence behind him is the purest he's ever heard. He hates himself. He knows if he turns he'll see the kid's lip aquiver, the eyes gleaming. Add one more crapslap to the worst day of his life. He strings the glove onto his belt. He walks on . . . and suddenly Kiki is yelling: "Jacklookout!"

His cap is gone! His head smacked and his cap gone! Gone with the devil girl's yell:

"Hi-yo, Hazel!"

JUBILEE

How could she resist? There he was, walking ahead of her. So tempting. So easy. She waves the cap grandly, flings it across the Plains as she flung the glove, races on.

She happens upon girls playing football. As soon as they spot her, they abandon the game and come running.

"Jubilee! Wow!"

"Hey! Is that what I think it is?"

"It *is*! It's Jack's!"

"Scramjet!"

"Omygod, Ace! How'd you get it?"

"Omygod omygod—look at her face! She *stole* it!"

"You da chick!"

She lets the fuss wash over her. When it subsides and they're all fish-eyed waiting for her to speak, she gives her patented little sniff and grin and says primly, "It's Hazel now."

Pandemonium. If somebody had a chisel and stone, they'd make a statue of her right here and now.

The girls circle, bend to huddle, cheer:

A—B—C—D—E—F—G!
Get these boy germs off of *me*!

As the huddle breaks and the din peters out, a voice calls: "C'mon, Ace, park it. We need a quarterback." A ball comes flying. She catches it and, as always, feels the loving seduction of the pigskin. Her fingers inchworm over the pebbled surface to the Chiclet-y laces. "Go!" she barks, and a dozen girls take off, looking back over their shoulders, calling her name, pleading. She picks one out, throws, leads her by a good twenty yards because she's arcing it high and is already peeling out before it comes down. It's not these girls she most has to see. It's someone else.

DESTROYER

THE FUN COMES TO AN END when the Big Kid rescue
squad shows up. They throw the life preserver to the
mortified victim, Henry. It's just an inner tube on a
rope. The kid grabs it for dear life, and they drag him
across the dust to safety and a riot of cheers—you'd
think the kid had just hit four home runs in a row. The
little kids begin to disperse, some of them, the boys,
back to their war games.

Destroyer grins. Other kids play war. To them it's a
game. Not to Destroyer. He's never fired a fake bullet,
never dropped a bogus bomb. His weapon is different

from all the others: it's real. Even though you can't see it, even though you can't touch it. But you sure can feel it. His weapon is fear. Destroyer understands fear. Understands it like he understands aloneness. He could never explain it in words. Perhaps his understanding began the day Daffy died. All he knows is, fear works. He believes that the source of fear lives in his pocket, in the yellow plastic clicker that he found one day in Stuff. He discovered that the clicker had power. He discovered that if he pointed it at a little kid and clicked it and said *"Bam!"* or *"Pow!"* or "You're dead!" the little kid would believe it—not play it but *believe* it. He gave the clicker a name: Exploder.

He's crouching by the truck now, out of sight of the kids streaming back to their play. Many are in pairs or groups, but here comes a solo runt in a striped shirt. Destroyer shows himself, calls "Hey." The kid turns, sees—and that's all it takes. His bugged-out eyes freeze on Destroyer's outstretched hand, on Exploder. He knows the drill. By now they all do. Three clicks and you're dead. Exploded. Smithereens. Destroyer doesn't even have to say *"Pow!"* anymore.

Click

Click

Click

The stiff yelps, lurches, falls backward, lies sputtering on the ground.

Destroyer ambushes two more, a boy and a girl. Body count: three. Plus Henry. A good morning's work. He climbs into the truck. Sooner or later it will occur to the dumb clucks that they're not really dead. They'll get up and walk away. And when he sees them again, they'll *still* believe. Fear. It's the best beauty of Destroyer's weapon: it can kill you over and over.

He was going to stop but it's too much fun. He knows where to find more victims. Snuggle Stop. He rolls.

LAJO

Dᴜꜱᴛy ꜱᴛᴏᴘꜱ, points. "There she is!"

She's rounding Doll Farm, seems to be making a beeline for somewhere. Even at this distance LaJo can see that her legs are not moving. Already she knows what it took Jack months to learn: there is little need to pedal Scramjet. If *fast* is what you want, all you have to do is give a light heeltap to the chain, hold out your feet and pull down your hat.

"C'mon!" Dusty takes off after her. Like he's really going to catch her on foot.

There's an empty swing nearby. LaJo takes a seat.

There's something he's been wanting to do since they met up with Jack at the tracks. Wanting but not wanting. Because he's afraid of what he might see. Or not see. He stares at the faraway rider, her ponytail straight out, and Dusty's stupid pursuit. A Sillynilly comes screaming down a sliding board. . . .

Do it.

He does it. Doesn't think, just does it. Pulls up his shirt and looks . . . and almost faints with relief. It's there, plain, clear, sharp as always. The tattoo. The inky eye in the middle of his stomach. Same as everyone's . . . everyone's except . . .

For the tenth time LaJo flashes to the moment back at the tracks. Jack lifting his shirt to wipe his face, LaJo seeing it, the sudden nameless chill between his shoulder blades: *Jack's tattoo is fading!*

JUBILEE

SPINNING SPOKES DICE SUNBEAMS, spit diamonds: Jubilee rides.

Along the way girls cheer:

"Go, Jubilee!"

"You da girl!"

"Doin it—yeah!"

Boys stare stunned, sullen.

She ripples through the hoed rows of Doll Farm, little mothers pulling up their rubbery babies naked as turnips, shaking dirt loose from round, astonished eyes. She verves and swerves through Thousand

Puddles for a bit, then thinks *Heck with it* and slices the rest of them down the middles. When she sees the DON'T sign coming up, she's tempted—oh she's tempted, because there's nothing she can't do today, nothing, and the sign is so flimsy, just posterboard on a stick and the hand-lettered word. So easy to snatch. She reaches, reaches . . . but at the last instant veers off with a laugh.

Approaching Snuggle Stop, she slows down. Her memories of the candy-cane-striped red-and-white hut are still warm. Many days she stood in line with the other little kids, awaiting her turn to step inside and lose herself in the big, soft, loving, furry embrace of Snugger. To this day neither she nor anyone else knows what Snugger looks like, it's so dark in there. Not that it matters. All that matters is that Snugger is there to give you what you need, whenever, 24/7. She feels the need less now. Only rarely is Snuggle Stop visited by a Big Kid, and then only at night, a solitary shadow crabbing over the glittery landscape, cursing the moon that is always full over Hokey Pokey.

It has been one of the quiet prides of Jubilee's life that her little brother, Albert, has never stood in the line at Snuggle Stop. He hasn't had to, because she sees to it that he goes to sleep snuggled into the loving spoon of his big sister and wakes up the same way.

Until this morning.

She reins in Hazel. She surveys the long line. There he is, toward the end, in his striped shirt. His posture alone tells her all she needs to know. A sob ball falls from her. It's the saddest thing she's ever seen. She hates herself.

She parks the bike. She moves closer. She calls, "Albert." He looks—oh the look! He turns away. She says his name again.

He turns. He wails, "You wasn't there!"

Now or never, she thinks. She reaches for him, tugs. He resists. Then doesn't. He allows her to pull him away from the line. She needs to distract him, make him forget. She points to the bike. "Look, Albert— want a ride?"

Albert looks, then kicks her in the shin. "You wasn't there."

She fights the tears. Abandoning him to wake up alone, choosing bike over brother—is there a rottener sister anywhere? "I know, I know, I'm sorry."

"And then I got exploded!"

She looks at him. "Huh?"

"I got exploded!" he bawls. "And I was nex!"

She cups his shoulders. "What are you talking about?"

"I was nex in line and then he did it!"

"Who? What?"

He snivels: "I was nex in line for Snugger and Destroyer came in his truck and exploded me and when I was dead the other kids went ahead of me and then I was at the end of the line!" He kicks her again.

She's not sure what all that's about. She only knows she needs to steer him in a new direction. She leads him to the bike. "Look, Albert—it's mine now. Want to ride?"

He looks at it. He won't give up his monkey face, but she can see a glimmer. He reaches out, pulls his hand back and kicks the front tire. The bike topples. "You wasn't there!" She catches the bike before it hits the ground. He's bawling harder than ever now.

She picks him up, pulls him into herself. She's not furry and her name's not Snugger, but she gives him the best, the warmest, the most loving hug a sister ever gave a kid brother. She sobs into his ear. "I'm sorry, honeybunny, I know, I know. Bad Jubilee. Bad. Bad. She'll never do it again. Never let you wake up alone again, never, never, *never*." And suddenly she's aware that he's clutching—*Thank you!*—his arms and legs wrapped around her, practically squeezing the breath out of her. Then a shift in his weight. He's reaching over her shoulder, reaching for the bike—

She lets him down. She lets him pet it. She kneels behind him, chin on his shoulder. He's still sniffing but she knows the worst is over. He's drinking in the full glorious view. "So—what do you think?"

He traces his fingers solemnly over the black-and-silver flanks. "Where'd you get it?"

"Oh, it just sort of came to me." Get him off this track. "I call her Hazel."

"It's Scramjet," he says matter-of-factly. "It's Jack's."

Why is she surprised? Jack and Scramjet are famous, even among little kids, *especially* among little kids.

"Not anymore. It's Hazel." She kisses his ear, whispers into it. "And it's *mine*."

No reaction, but she knows he's taking it in, processing. His eyes never leave the bike.

"And y'know what?"

"What?"

"I think Hazel wants a new paint job."

At first there's no sign, and she's afraid he's missed it. But now his head is turning, and one wide, wonderstruck eye is coming into view. . . .

JACK

EVERYBODY KNOWS. Everybody's a detective.

"Hey, Jack! I saw her over there!"

"Hey, Jack! Over there!"

"Hey, Jack! I saw bike tracks!"

"Hey, Jack! We're makin a posse! We'll find her!"

So public his shame. For once, he resents his own popularity. Every show of sympathy, every offer to help, cranks up his disgrace, his hatred of the girl.

"Hey, Jack! We found Scramjet!"

Jack waves dismissively: *Yeah, right.*

"Jack! It's *buried*!"

He halts. Frost coats his heart. *Would she?*

It's a couple of Gappergums, a girl and a boy, pulling up in front of him, panting. He knows they have no more sense than moss, so why is he listening?

"Behind Tantrums, Jack! Mitchell found it!" Each grabs a hand. "C'mon!"

Jack allows himself to be led. Prays: *Please no*. But fears.

As they head for Tantrums, Jack is barely aware of walking through Flowers, barely aware that, midmorning, it's already trampled. Two Snotsippers and a Longspitter are waiting in line to enter Tantrums. All three are grimly tearing at faceless rag dolls, ripping them to shreds: dog bones for fitpitchers. On a bench outside the door sits a bored Big Kid, the attendant. His job is to hand out rag dolls and assist the exiting fitpitcher, who often can hardly walk at the end of his or her tantrum. Tantrums itself is a dome-shaped structure—white, rubbery, soundproof—with a plastic pipe in the top for tantrum exhaust. The color of the exhausting gas signifies tantrum category, from One (black: mild) to Five (white: achieved only once, by Robert the Fuse). At the moment it's showing aqua: Category Three.

From behind Tantrums comes a cry: "I need help!"

They run. Mitchell, a Longspitter, is tugging a bike wheel, still half buried, and at once Jack's heartfrost melts: it's not Scramjet. It can't be. It's too big. Mitchell is grunting with effort. Jack, feeling charitable now, grabs Mitchell's spade, pushes him aside. "You need to dig more." A couple minutes of spadework frees the wheel. Jack lifts it, stands it on the ground. The little kids gasp, wonderwowed, reach tentatively to touch it. They've never seen anything like it. Neither has Jack. Half the spokes are gone. All remaining metal is a rock-hard red-brown rustcrust. All that remains of the rubber are a few black scraps. But that's not what astounds them—it's the size. The wheel stands higher than Jack's head.

"Jack," one croaks, "what is it?"

"What it looks like," says Jack. "A bike wheel."

"*That* big?"

"Yeah." Dumb answer, but that's all he can say, for he has no idea where it came from or what it's doing in the ground. He's heard of a race of giant bikes that once roamed the land, but he's always assumed it was a fairy tale.

Suddenly he stops—that sound again. He turns.

"Who whistled?" They look at him like he's goofy. Already Mitchell is back to digging.

As Jack walks away, he hears Mitchell's cry: "Sprocket!"

He passes Tantrums again. The Big Kid attendant is helping a sagging fitpitcher wobble off as, already, the next in line plunges inside and slams the door.

He spots the tiny terrorist, the one who calls himself Destroyer. He's pointing his plastic clicker at a pair of little kids dumb enough to believe it's a magic weapon. Normally Jack would sneak over behind the kid, mess with him somehow, show him up for the harmless runt he really is. But he's got no will for it today. Everything's been sucked out of him but the need to get his bike back.

A gang of assorted little ones comes running. "Hey, Jack!" He keeps walking, tries to ignore them. It doesn't work. They plant themselves in front of him. "Jack! Jack!"

He blows disgust, snarls: "What?"

"Jack—is there monsters?" pipes one, pulling on his pant leg. "There is, right, Jack? Right?"

"No there ain't!" screams another. "Tell him, Jack! There ain't no such thing as monsters!"

Now they're all babbling, pushing, clutching at him.

"Yes there is!"

"No there ain't!"

"Jack! Jack!"

Over their heads he spots Dusty and LaJo. He pushes through the kids—"Whatever"—tries to move on, but they practically trip him clinging to his legs. "Jack! Tell us! Tell us!"

He shakes them off, rudely shoves the most persistent one away. But already they're regrouping. He points, warns: "Touch me again—" They stop in their tracks. He's heard the question many times before and has always, according to his whim, snapped off a sharp yes or no and enjoyed the victors' cheers and the losers' glum dejection. But he's in no mood to play this time, so for once he'll give them the only honest answer there is, unsatisfying as it may be to all, which of course is, *How the heck do I know?*—when all of a sudden, out of nowhere, there they are, the words, the *real* answer, coming out of his mouth: "You believe there is, there is. You believe there ain't, there ain't." Jack leaves them staring stupidly at him like guppies in a fishbowl, musing as he walks away, *Where did that come from?*

The Amigos are heading away from him. They don't seem to have noticed him.

"Hey!" he calls.

They keep walking.

"Amigos!"

They keep walking. It's not like they're miles away. He knows they hear him. What's going on? He feels the chill coming on again.

He trots, calls: "Dusty! LaJo!"

They don't turn till he's practically up their backs. "Hey, Jack," they go, acting surprised, but it's fake, and so are the smiles.

"So?" he says. His mouth is dry. He hardly gets out the next word. "Anything?"

They trade glances. "Hey, no," says Dusty, like, *What a silly question.*

Neither will meet his eyes. Something tells him, *Walk away. Don't ask.* But he does. "What is it? Stop lying. What happened?"

Dusty is trying so hard he's squeaking. "Nothing happened, Jackarooni. We're still looking."

Jack grabs a fistful of shirt, pulls Dusty to his toes. "What?"

LaJo says, "It's painted."

For a moment the world stops. "Huh?"

"Yellow."

Dusty yells, "Shut up, you moron!"

LaJo shrugs. "He'll find out anyway. He should hear it from us."

The word has long since passed through his outer ear, speared the drum and inner ear; now it burrows deeper, deeper into his brain—and still makes no sense.

Yellow?

JUBILEE

OF COURSE HE WANTS TO—what kid wouldn't want to ride Scramjet (oops, Hazel) by himself, and she's proud that he wants to—but Albert's little legs are way too short to reach the pedals. So she walks alongside, holding him to the saddle, while he churns his legs in the air. "C'mon, Jubilee! Faster!" The paint is still wet. By now her little brother is half yellow himself but couldn't care less—he's riding the most famous bike in all the world! "Faster!"

She trots. His arms are stretched to their limit to reach the handlebar. It's getting harder to keep him safe and under control because he's turning the front wheel this way and that, pretending he's swooping over Great Plains chasing the wild herd. He's been delirious ever since she gave him the paintbrush. In spite of herself she winced as he slapped yellow even on the spokes and tires, but her heart is singing to know she's made him so happy, and there's no way she's going to stop him.

"Faster!"

She accelerates.

"Faster!"

She goes as fast as she dares. She's holding one slippery yellow handlegrip now as he thrusts both hands in the air and yells at boggle-eyed watchers: "Look at me! Look at me! I'm Jack!"

AMIGOS

"Did you see it?"

"What?"

"You know what."

"I saw *something*. But the sun was in my eyes. It mighta been sun glare."

"It wasn't sun. It was real."

They're talking about the uncomfortablest moment of their lives, the moment after they told Jack they had spotted Scramjet. When LaJo told him it was yellow, Jack seemed confused, as if he needed a dictionary to look up the word. "*Yellow?*" he said. Then his face, his whole body, seemed to crumple. He slumped to the ground at their feet and began to cry. He pulled up his shirt to hide his face—and that's when Dusty saw it too. And that's when they walked away, left him alone.

"Say it," says LaJo.

"Say what?" says Dusty.

"Say it."

Dusty has had his back turned to LaJo the whole time. "Say *what*?"

LaJo doesn't answer. He knows Dusty can't stand silence. If nobody else fills it, he will.

Dusty kicks dirt, picks a weed, chews it, spits it out, slumps, sighs dramatically, throws his hands to the sky: "O-K. His tattoo."

"His tattoo what?"

Dusty turns. His eyes are glistening. He seems to be looking for something that LaJo can't give him. He creaks, disbelieving: "It's . . . *fading*."

LaJo says vacantly, "It's almost gone."

Dusty surrenders, sags, sighs, nods.

They share a long silence that even Dusty does not invade. At last LaJo says, "So. What do you think?"

Dusty drags his eyes skyward. He gives a LaJo-like shrug. "I don't know."

"I didn't say *know*. I said *think*. What do you *think*?"

Dusty tries, tries, gives up, snarls: "I don't think nothin. Nothin. OK?" More silence. Kicking dust. Staring at separate horizons. Dusty turns, stares at LaJo. Suddenly he lifts his own shirt. He can't stand to look. "Is it there?"

LaJo looks. "It's there."

Dusty blows relief, checks out his tattoo. It's clear and sharp as always. The unblinking inky eye. The belly-button eyeball staring at all there is. A bold stare. A daring stare. "Lift your shirt," he says to LaJo. "Let me check you."

"I'm OK," says LaJo.

"How do you know?"

"I checked."

"You checked? Why?"

"I already knew about Jack. I saw him at the tracks."

Dusty screeches. "What? You saw him? You didn't say nothin? You didn't tell me?"

"I wasn't sure. Till I saw it again."

Dusty tromps in agitated circles, faces LaJo. "So what do *you* think?"

LaJo takes a long time to answer. "I think something's gonna happen."

Dusty goes into a fit of blinking, as if blinking can erase what was said. "*Something?* What's *something?* What's *that* s'pose to mean? Something *what?*"

"You're squeaking."

Dusty kicks a stone at LaJo. He walks off as if he's never coming back, comes back, snaps, "When?"

"When what?"

"When's this *something* gonna happen? Whatever it is."

LaJo shrugs. "I don't know." He lets out a long breath. "All I know is the tattoo is fading. Nobody else's is. Not yours. Not mine. Only his. It's fading. I don't know what it means neither. Except something's gonna happen." He looks off. "Soon."

Dusty shrieks: *"Soon?"*

LaJo shrugs. "It's fading fast. So . . . soon. You ain't gotta be Einstein."

The moment has become too hot. They back off, stare emptily at little kids kicking a soccer ball around. LaJo nods beyond. "Look."

It's the runty hellion, the walking explosion, on his haunches, watching the ballkickers.

"That's the kid that did it," says Dusty.

"Did what?"

"Dumped a Newbie into Socks. Didn't you hear it?"

"Guess not."

"Then he went to Snuggle Stop and messed with kids in line."

"Reg'lar maniac."

"Let's go mess him up."

LaJo stares.

Neither moves.

"Snugger," says Dusty. He grins. "Little kids love that dude."

So do you, you big baby, LaJo thinks. *You sneak over at night. You think we don't know? You think we don't see you jump in with little kids and do the hokey pokey?*

Silence. Eyes too bright. Corked panic. "Who's Einstein?" says Dusty.

DESTROYER

I AM THE LION. They are the zebras. They're nervous. They keep their eyes on me even while they're kicking the ball. They wonder which one of them I'm gonna go after, gonna eat. They blubber: "Please don't let it be me!" The joke is, I'm staying right here, enjoying myself. Making them nervous is just as much fun as eating them. Well, almost. Well, lookie lookie, here comes the ball rolling towards me. And look—nobody's coming after it. They're just standing there like dopes. Look at them flinch as I stand up. They think I'm gonna take their ball. Or come after them. But I'm not. I'm just gonna turn and walk away, turn and walk away and go back to the other lions and tell them about it and we'll all roll on our backs in the grass and laugh big roary lion laughs.

JACK

"GOT THE GRUMPIES, Jack?"

Jack unfunks slowly, finds himself straddling one end of the seesaw. How did he get to Playground? Lopez looks down from the high end, the dirty bottoms of her dangling feet a darker shade of herself. Lopez spends half her life on the low end of the seesaw, too small to push herself up, waiting for a weightier kid to take the other end, supply the power. It's usually a futile wait. It takes a Big Kid—jumping—to reach and pull down the high empty end, and most Big Kids have no time for tots and seesaws. But not Jack. He's always got a minute for Lopez, tickled to hear her squeals as his downpush sends her skyward.

He peers at her up the length of the gray plank. "Huh?"

"Got the grumpies, Jack?"

He nods dopily. He resents her dragging him out of oblivion. *What kinda stupid question is that?* he wants to say.

"Bad day, Jack?"

She's tipped forward, leaning hard into the hand bar, both terrified and thrilled to be hanging so high, not coming down. He remembers Kiki's trembling lip. "I guess," he says.

"Oh," she goes with a sad sag. She mulls, then: "So it's a bad day for me too, Jack."

Jack is about to say *Don't you ever compare your bad day with mine* when he realizes he's misunderstood her. She's trying to tell him she feels his pain. And indeed it shows on her little face. She's not acting. Despite himself, he is touched.

"Thanks, Lopee," he says, and pushes himself up, sending her—"Wheee!"—down. Useless as counterweight, she butt-bounces off the ground and shoots right back up, leaving Jack no more than a moment at the top—which is, next to Gorilla Hill, the second-highest point on Hokey Pokey. In that moment Jack sees it all: Great Plains and the rolling dustball of the wild herd, Trucks, Tantrums, The Kid, Hippodrome, the DON'T sign, Stuff, the red bluff and jungle treetops beyond and kids big and little everywhere streaking, leaping, chasing, shrieking, warring, hopscotching, footballing, hide-and-seeking, jumproping, hokeypoking, razzing, dazzing, runamucking, chuckleducking—all in full play now well into the sunny day that never really ends but is merely interrupted by the unwelcome arrival of night.

Jack has always loved these panoramic, top-of-the-plank snapshots of the world. It's one of the reasons he likes to seesaw Lopez. But this time . . . this time, as he sinks slowly back down, he is aware that something at the top was different. The world looked exactly the same as always—the places, the kids—but this time there was a slippery sense, like an uncatchable moth, that he himself was no longer part of the picture, was on the outside looking in, that the world he was seeing was no longer his. For a scary instant he thought his end of the seesaw was going to keep on rising and catapult him clear out of Hokey Pokey.

Lopez, hanging on, hovering, surveys the world. He speaks up to her: "Not just bad."

She turns away from the spectacular view, looks down at him, her little eyebrows pinched with concern. "Badder than bad, Jack?"

"Different," he says. "*Bad*'s not the word."

"What *is* the word, Jack?" Intensely curious.

He looks about, as if to find the word in the dust. "I don't know. *Strange*, maybe?"

She tastes it. "*Strange?*"

He shakes his head—"No . . . not . . ."—knows it's hopeless. "I don't think there is a word."

Lopez laughs, is so into her own laughter she doesn't notice she's shaking the high end. "Yeah there is, Jack. There's a word for everything. You just don't want to say it to me 'cause you think I'm little."

He can't explain, even to himself, so he reaches for something solid. "She stole my bike." It takes a moment to register. She gapes at him, speechless. He fires the other barrel. "She painted it."

Lopez practically falls off her perch, recovers, squeals: "Painted your *bike? Your* bike? *Scramjet?*"

Jack is grimly pleased. Little as she is, Lopez is normally hard to surprise. "Yeah," he says. "Yellow."

Lopez is twisting in her seat, scanning, thrusting her finger now. "Jack! Jack! There it is! She's riding it! Way over there!"

Jack pushes up, glimpses the yellow streak from the top before bouncing back to the ground.

"What are you gonna do, Jack?"

I'm gonna sit down and cry, he thinks. *Nope. Already did that. I'll go to Tantrums. I'll make Robert the Fuse seem like a peeper. I'll catch her . . . I'll catch her and I'll . . . She'll wish she was never . . .*

The question flies to the Mountains, echoes: *What are you gonna do, Jack?*

I'm gonna die, because there's no such thing as life without my bike.

Echoes: *What are you gonna do, Jack?*

"Catch the train."

That was weird. He imagines he just said *Catch the train.*

Lopez is laughing. "What's funny?" he says.

"You just said 'Catch the train,' Jack."

He stares at her. "I did?"

"Yeah, you did. There's no train, Jack. Just tracks. Everybody knows *that*." She giggles some more.

What's wrong with me?

He's woozy. The plank is getting rubbery. He hears himself laughing along, showing her he's just being silly. But she's stopped laughing now, she's giving him a new look, a look he can't read. He wants to make the

85

look go away, wants to make Lopez happy again. He pushes off the ground, sends himself up, her down, and at the top he shouts, "Look, Lopee—no hands!" and he releases the hand bar and thrusts his hands to the sky as he bounces back down. But her shriek of delight never comes. From her high perch she's gaping wide-eyed at him and the look is now unmistakable: it's pure shock. She points. "Jack! Your *tattoo*!"

For a moment he's puzzled, then realizes his shirt must have ridden up his stomach during his no-hands descent. Straddling the seat, he looks down at his white cotton T-shirt and suddenly knows he doesn't want to do it. The shadow of the brown bird flits across the gray plank. He pinches the hem of the shirt between a thumb and forefinger and slowly lifts. He gasps. His tattoo, the open eye, identical to that of every other kid in Hokey Pokey, is down to a couple of eyelashes and a gray smudge where the sharp dime of the eyeball used to be. It's all but gone. And he hears that sound again. A whistle.

Next thing he knows, he's on his butt in the dust and someone is calling, "Hey, Jack! Look what we got!"

AMIGOS

DUSTY CAN'T FIGURE OUT what he's looking at. On the one hand, Jack wobbles and tumbles comically backward from his seat on the seesaw; on the other hand, little Lopez, before she drops down, was definitely not laughing, not with that look on her face. Whatever. Dusty crackles with news and nothing is going to stop him, especially not LaJo, who refused to help and now glumps along twenty feet behind. "Hey, Jack!" Dusty calls. "Look what we got!"

Jack doesn't turn around, just sits in the dust. Maybe he doesn't hear. Dusty comes alongside. "Jack, look."

Heavily, as if his head weighs too much, Jack turns. His face is pale. His eyes land on the bike but somehow don't seem to see it. Dusty pats its rump. "It's a new bike, Amigo."

Jack doesn't respond. He seems to be in a fog. "We cut it from the herd. Well, I did."

It's old. Slow. "Hey"—he buddyclamps Jack's shoulder—"listen, I ain't saying we're giving up on Scramjet. We'll get it back, Jack, we'll get it back. I'm just saying, hey, it don't hurt to have a backup, right? Plan B. Just in case." He ignores LaJo's background slur—"It's a nag"—plows on: "We can fix it, dude. Clean this baby up. Shine 'er up." Even as he pats the lopsided saddle, a spring falls off. "We'll paint it, Jack. Black. Just like Scramjet. Maybe stripes!"

Jack is on his feet, walking away.

"You can call it Scramjet Two, Jack!" Dusty calls. "Waddaya think? Huh?"

They watch Jack go off, wanting to follow but leery. "I told you he didn't want it, ya dumb turdbrain," says LaJo.

"We can paint it," Dusty says weakly, more to himself than anyone else.

LaJo wags his head. "Let it go."

"No." Dusty's answer comes fast and firm, but when

LaJo lifts his hand from the bike's rump, Dusty doesn't resist. LaJo gives a gentle push, sending the creaking, leaking nag off in the general direction of Great Plains.

They watch Jack. Dusty's eyes brim. "I just thought—"

LaJo waves him off. "Forget it."

Jack's slumpshouldered figure recedes. The boys feel a vague unwinding, themselves helpless spindles.

"He knows," says LaJo.

"What?" says Dusty absently. Then, turning, startled: "*What?*"

"He saw it."

Dusty blinks a rainbow: tears, sun. As always, little kids are coming up to Jack, tugging, pestering, asking to play, but he ignores them. "You think?"

"Yeah."

Dusty squints after Jack. His lips move with unspoken words. He scuffs off, kicks dirt, picks up a stone, throws it, returns to LaJo. "What . . . what . . ." LaJo turns aside, Dusty pulls him back. His eyes are bright. "What's going on?" LaJo shrugs. Dusty grabs his shirt, wrenches. "*Huh?*"

LaJo sends Dusty reeling with a shove. "What do I look like, the freakin answer man?" He stomps to the seesaw and jerks down the high end, sending Lopez and her running nose on her quickest up and down ever.

JUBILEE

DROPS ALBERT OFF at Cartoons. Up on the giant outdoor screen twenty-foot-tall Sylvester the Cat is chasing Tweety Bird. So what's new? Kids on trikes mob the front, Albert's favorite place, so he heads back to the walkers and in a moment disappears among the cross-legged grass-sitters. Jubilee turns and pedals off.

The first thing she did after getting the bike was make a beeline for the tree hole and leave a note for Ana Mae: *Meet me at The Kid.* But then she got caught up in her joyride and Albert, and now she wonders if Ana Mae has bothered to wait this long.

She has. There she is, napping on the pedestal of the great statue, her back against The Kid's stony shin, her brimmed cap down over her face. The great outstretched arm and famously pointing finger appear to shelter her.

She calls: "Ana Mae!" Ana Mae's cap falls as she jerks awake, looks around. Her eyes locate Jubilee, lock in as Jubilee heads straight for her like a shot arrow, rumppumping and yelling "Yeeeeeee-haaaaaaaah!" In a swirl of dust the bike skidbrakes a one-eighty and comes to a stop directly beneath the stone finger, the front tire kissing her pal's sneaker toe.

Expecting boggle-eyed stupendiment, Jubilee is disappointed. Ana Mae is staring, but with nothing more than routine curiosity. "New bike?" she says. "You made me wait here for *this*?"

Jubilee remembers: the bike is yellow now. Ana Mae doesn't recognize it. "It's not just any bike," she says.

Ana Mae yawns. "Really."

Jubilee rolls the front tire lightly onto Ana Mae's sneaker top. She grins. "Gimme an S . . . gimme a C . . . gimme an R . . . gimme an A . . . gimme an M . . . gimme a J . . ."

And there it is: the boggle-eyed stupendiment, and more. Ana Mae is on her feet, cupping her face, screeching. *"Scramjet?"*

Jubilee gives a smuggy nod. "Hazel to you."

Ana Mae goes bananas, apples, kumquats. She screams, twirls, cartwheels. This is what Jubilee loves most about bestfriendship: when something great happens to one, it happens to both. She kickstands Hazel and joins the celebration. They do their special fingermess handslap, their special shimmyshakejive buttbump. Ana Mae thrusts her arms toward the bike: *"Yellow?"*

"Albert did it!"

More howls. The girls drop to their knees and bow grandly to the bike as if to a Supreme Sultan of All. They squat like linebackers, bark into each other's faces:

> *Boys! Boys! They're worse than toys!*
> *They're only good*
> *For making noise!*

They hold hands and dance around the bike. Again Ana Mae pulls away. She's beginning to think. Jubilee has known it was coming. Jack and Scramjet were like peanut butter and jelly. So familiar were they, so often together, they seemed like a single two-wheeled creature. Some even gave them one name: Scramjack. No wonder the disbelief in Ana Mae's eyes. No wonder the question coming. But Jubilee isn't ready to answer it yet, if she even knows the answer, so when Ana Mae says, hands imploring, "How . . . like . . . *how?* . . ."

Jubilee waves it off and changes the subject: "How, schmow—who cares?" She kicks up the stand, offers a handlebar. "Here. Take 'er for a spin."

Ana Mae goes into shock. She backs up, stares at the bike, stammers: "Will he . . . she . . . *let* me? I thought only Jack could . . ."

Jubilee rolls the bike up to Ana Mae. "Girl, look at me. Do I look like Jack?" She takes Ana Mae's hand and wraps her fingers around a grip. She lets go so Ana Mae has no choice but to take control of the bike. There's a brief shudder in the flank, a faint snort, but that's all. "Go . . . go," says Jubilee. Ana Mae, always the more emotional of the two, is sobbing. If Jubilee lets this nonsense go on any longer, she's going to start bawling too. She jerks Ana Mae's leg off the ground, hoists it over the saddle and onto the farside pedal and smacks her shoulder. "Go!"

With a deep sigh and the plaintive whimper that

precedes a plunge into the unknown, Ana Mae pushes off. Within moments she's yipping like a crazed cowgirl and framing The Kid in widening circles of dust ruts. She gives Jubilee a start when, briefly, she gallops so far she's out of sight, but she comes roaring back and skids to a halt, flush-faced and gasping, "Hey—why stop with yellow? Let's girl it up some more!"

So they do. They head off to Stuff's rumpled dump, and before long the bike is sparkling with glitter, pink ribbons stream from pink handlegrips, the saddle has a white fuzzy cover, HAZEL is painted on left and right flanks, and a string of pink and white bunnytail pom-poms gives the rear end a tail that flies straight out at full speed.

Ana Mae perches clapping atop the sliding board as Jubilee zips and skitters through Playground. Little kids drop like apples from monkey bars and swings and come running. Jubilee pulls up, rears her mount on its hind tire and twirls the front. Frenzy grips the crowd. Jubilee thrusts a fist to the sky. "Hail Hazel!" she cries, and a hundred little girlfists shoot skyward and the mobdin echoes, "Hail Hazel!"

JACK

FINDS HIMSELF STANDING in a patch of soil: Flowers. He looks down. White and yellow blooms are flattened beneath his feet. In the distance he hears cries of "Hail Hazel!" He shivers. He wonders where the cold is coming from. He doesn't want to move. Not ever again.

But he does. Somehow he lifts a foot, then another, and leaves the patch behind and wanders . . . wanders . . .

The world is rushing at him, confusing him, alarming him. The whispered voice in his ear. Scramjet. The sound no one else hears. It's a train whistle—he knows that now. But it makes no sense—no train ever comes to Hokey Pokey. The looks on the faces of LaJo and Dusty and Lopez. The feeling that has no name, as if he's being poured from a bottle. The giant fossilized wheel and sprocket. But most of all the horror under his shirt. He is tempted to look again. Maybe it was a hallucination. Maybe the eye is clear and sharp and complete as ever. But he doesn't really believe that. He doesn't look because he's afraid it may have faded even more.

What's happening?
What does it all mean?

He doesn't know. He doesn't want to know. He only wants things to be the way they were. Cruising Hokey Pokey on Scramjet. Tarzancalling his Amigos. Tossing grounders to Kiki. Seesawing Lopez. Cruising and playing and laughing all the sun long in a shower of shouts: "Hey, Jack! Hey, Jack!" Cartoony noises come to him dimly: the endless squabble of Sylvester and Tweety Bird. "I tawt I taw a putty tat. I did! I did! . . ."

Sun. Dust. Sun. Dust.

it's . . . time

JUBILEE

THEY'VE BEEN CRUISING AROUND, or, as Ana Mae likes to say, pokin the Hokey. Now they're doing one of their favorite things: picking blackberries.

And Ana Mae is laughing. "You're *jealous!*"

Jubilee has just told Ana Mae about Albert shouting "I'm Jack!" as he rode Hazel, which he persisted in calling Scramjet. Already Jubilee regrets she said anything. She laughs back. "Jealous? *Not.*"

Ana Mae laughs harder.

"What?"

"You're so funny, Ace. You should see your face.

You're the world's worst actor. You"—she pops a berry into her mouth—"are jealous"—another pop—"of Jack."

Jubilee throws a berry at Ana Mae. "I am *not*!"

Ana Mae rolls her eyes, tosses up a berry, catches it in her mouth, sighs, "Whatever."

"Don't *whatever* me," Jubilee growls. "Listen to what you're saying. What's that supposed to mean— me, jealous? You think my little brother likes that . . . *male* . . . better than me? His own sister?"

"Hey, don't get your pants in a bunch." As a peace-making gesture, Ana Mae tosses a berry for Jubilee to mouth-catch. To show she's not ready for peace, Jubilee swats it away. So Ana Mae flips one to herself. "No big deal, Jubie Jube. Albert's a boy. Jack's a boy. Boys side with boys. So, like, what's new?"

Jubilee snaps, "Albert is *not* a boy. He's a brother. *Mine*."

Ana Mae gapes at her pal with open amusement, breaks out laughing. "Ace, girl, I think you're a little, like, confused?"

Jubilee's shock-face may or may not be fake—it's hard to tell. "Oh really? So first I'm jealous and now I'm confused."

Which sends Ana Mae into another howl. "I guess. You are one messed-up—" Before she lands on the word *chickie*, three blackberries pelt her face.

Jubilee sneers, "Say your prayers, girlfriend," and the berry fight is on.

Round the thorny tangle of berrywhips they go. Screaming. Laughing. Flinging. Trash-talking. Pickerpoke-yipping, "Ow! Ow!" Suddenly, as Ana Mae fires one over the thicket, Jubilee vanishes.

JACK

Wanders . . .

JUBILEE

ANA MAE CIRCLES the thicket warily, suspecting a trick, berries ready. It's not a trick. Jubilee is picking herself up from the ground. She's tripped in a hole. Her ammo lies scattered in the dust. She flexes her ankle. "Some little snotface was digging around here." As she says this, she spots something in the berry tangle. She reaches in carefully and pulls it out. It's a shovel. Red, metal, wooden handle.

With no digger to yell at, Jubilee glares angrily at the spade. She winds up and is about to heave it when she abruptly stops and pulls the spade in close. She inspects it. She knocks it against the ground. She stares off, blinking, thinking. She walks to the edge of the bluff.

"Jube, what—"

Jubilee is pointing. Ana Mae doesn't have to ask where. Across the tracks and the jungle to the creek. To the grassy, egg-shaped island in the creek. To Forbidden Hut on the island in the creek.

"Let's do it," says Jubilee.

Ana Mae groans. "What's the point? Nothing ever works."

But Jubilee is already slipsliding down the steep bluffside to the tracks, waving the spade, calling back: "I got a new idea!"

Ana Mae stuffs her unfired handful into her mouth. "Wait for me!"

JACK

WANDERS . . .

DESTROYER

Swaggers through Playground. Triple-clicks a few screaming Snotsippers and a Gappergum. High on the monkey bars two Groundhog Chasers snicker and go back to their business. He points Exploder at the black-haired girl on the down end of the seesaw.

Click

The girl laughs.

Click

Click

Click

Now the girl gets serious, puts a look of shock on her face, throws her arms into the air and falls backward off her seat. She lies spread-eagle on the ground, croaking, "He got me . . . he got me . . . I'm dead. . . ." He's not sure what to make of her. She's playing along, but it's not playing along that he wants. He wants believers. Real prey. Victims.

He puts away Exploder. From another pocket he pulls his slingshot. The remaining Snotsippers scream and take off. The Groundhog Chasers, upside down now and watching him, reach into their own pockets. Time to vamoose.

Search and destroy.

Ammo is plentiful: stones on the ground. He fires at passing pedal-trucks. At Jailhouse. At abandoned dolls. He passes under the outstretched arm of The Kid. He thinks about it, decides he better not.

The brown bird is flying overhead. He fires. Misses. He can't remember ever hitting it.

He's so hungry for targets he takes aim at his own shadow. But the sun is high and his shadow just a slim tide in front of him. He hits his foot. "Ow!"

Where are groundhogs when you need them? Maybe he can spot one from the bluff. He heads over there.

JACK

ON GREAT PLAINS. Not alone. Surrounded by mustangs. He has wandered into the midst of the wild herd. They stand facing the four directions. A muted nicker here, a shudder of flank there—otherwise a stillness so perfect they might be posing for a picture. So why aren't they running? Can't they see him? Is he a ghost? Invisible? He claps his hands, shouts "Hey!" The herd bolts as one, scattershot, regroups, boils dust for the Mountains.

Alone now. He wishes they would come back. He wishes yesterday would come back. A tumbleweed rolls over his foot, rolls on. Even the tumbleweed seems to know where it is, where it's going. Calibrated to ride, his muscles misfire. They grope for the wheel turn, but there is no wheel. The soles of his feet feel the pedal's press, but there is no pedal.

He senses something behind. He turns. Nothing. His eyes skim the scruff of Great Plains and Tantrums and Cartoons and come to rest on The Kid, the statue commanding even at this distance. Something is different. It takes a moment for Jack to realize what it is. All his life The Kid has been pointing toward the creek and the tracks. Now he's pointing this way. Or is Jack imagining things again? No. And he's not just pointing this way, he's pointing directly, unmistakably, at Jack himself. "No!" he shouts at the finger, and sprints a hundred yards to the left. He looks. The finger is still on him, dead center. He turns his back on it. Thunder rumbles beyond the Mountains. He falls to his knees. He scoops handfuls of dirt, flings them into the air and cries out, "NOOOOOOOOOOOO!" as the bitter dust of Hokey Pokey rains down upon his head.

JUBILEE

THEY RACE DOWN THE TRACKS, veer left through the jungle and burst onto the narrow, pebbled beach of the creek. A gang of kids is already on the island. They're lugging a ten-foot log. They back up to water's edge. Someone barks, "One! Two! Three!" and they advance, a many-legged kidderpillar lumbering toward the Hut. The log smashes into the door, bounces off. They back up and try again. Five times they try before giving up. They drop the log and stagger away, brushing bark from themselves. Some don't even bother to step on rocks as they slosh across the stream and slump past the girls into the jungle.

Jubilee needles: "Strike out, boys?"

JACK

It comes to him with such force, such simple clarity, that he cries it aloud: "Tattooer!"

He's Jack. Say it again: He's Jack! Jack does not give up. Jack does not wimp out. Jack battles. He will go to Tattooer, get a new one. He will track the girl and get his bike back. Repaint it better than ever. This thing that is happening, whatever it is, he will dehappen it. He will drag this day, pummel this day, back to normal.

Start with Kiki. He finds him at Cartoons, cross-legged in the grass, gaping up at the great screen.

"Kiki!" he calls. Kiki turns. The joy on his face tells Jack his earlier meanness has been long forgotten. Kiki snatches his glove and comes running, untied laces flapping. "Hey, Jack! Hey, Jack!" Kiki pulls up, tongue hanging, panting. The kid is so puppy-like Jack sometimes fears he'll jump up and start licking him in the face.

"Got your new ball?" says Jack. He prays the kid found it after the unkind kick across the Plains.

The kid pulls the black-taped ball from his mitt. "Right here."

"Give," says Jack. Kiki flips him the ball. He deloops his own glove from his belt. "OK, let's go."

They fall into their routine as neatly as a foot slipping into an old sneaker. They move without measurement to positions precisely twenty steps from each other, facing. Kiki readies himself: knees bent, weight on toes, arms hanging, poised.

"Say it," says Jack.

Kiki barks: "Eyes on the ball."

"What?"

"Eyes on the ball!"

Jack tosses the ball once, twice, in his bare hand, getting the feel. He rolls a grounder, slow, directly at Kiki. The kid snaps it up, sidewinds it back. More slow, easy ones. Now a few to the left. The right. Rolling them faster now. Faster. The kid handles them all, shifting nimbly to throwing position even as he plucks them from the dust. Jack grins to see the kid's tongue poke out each time a ball comes. Jack feels a swell of pride. He's taught the kid well.

Fly balls now, sending the kid back, left, right. The last one is always the same: Jack rears back and fires one straight up as hard as he can. He puts so much into it he's sometimes surprised the ball doesn't bounce off the sky. Jack's favorite part is the kid's reaction, a strung-out yelp of wonder and delight as the ball, at its peak, shrinks to the size of a pea. Fright sweetens the yelp as the ball descends, getting bigger, faster. The kid circles, staggers drunkenly and finally emits a faint squeak of surprise as the ball plops into his outstretched mitt.

As always, the kid comes running, waving the ball. "I caught it!"

Jack rewards him with a nod. He is careful not to overpraise the kid, give him a big head.

The kid is panting, more from excitement than exhaustion. "How'd I do, Jack? Huh?"

Jack pretends to think it over, flips the kid a crumb: "Not bad."

The kid beams.

JUBILEE

THE GIRLS ROCKWALK across the water to the island. Jubilee foots the abandoned log and with a dismissive sniff rolls it into the creek. They stand before Forbidden Hut. They behold it as one of the wonders, one of the great mysteries, of the world. No one knows who named it Forbidden. No one knows who made it or why it's here on this island in the creek. Or why it even exists at all. Most of all, no one knows what it looks like inside. Because no one has ever *been* inside. Not for lack of trying. Hardly a day goes by that someone doesn't try. The rocks are worn pearly by the feet of creek-crossers. The more kids can't get in, the more they want to. The pattern endlessly repeats: curiosity leads to determination leads to frustration leads to fury leads to sullen, sagging defeat. And simmering beneath all that: surprise.

Surprise, because getting in looks first off like a piece of cake. It's not like the Hut is a stone fortress or anything. Its windowless walls and flat roof are a patchwork of scraps that look like they came from Stuff: particleboard, shingles, bed slats. It looks like a kids' clubhouse. A cheesy one at that.

But surprise is not at the bottom of the bottom. Disappointment is. Sticky, won't-rub-off disappointment—because the Hut seems so inviting. It practically croons in the ear of everyone who sees it: *Come on in, kid. This is your place.* That's what hurts so much, that a place that seems to welcome you, a place that seems *made* for you, will not let you in.

Nothing is more ordinary-looking, or surprising, than the door. To look at it, it's just that: a door. A plain, white-painted (generously chipped) plywood door with a plain, ordinary, yo-yo-shaped brass doorknob. It looks as if all you have to do is turn the knob and—presto!—you're in. Forget it. That brassy knob is

113

polished to high gold by the hands of kids trying to turn it, trying to get in. Big Kids. Little kids. Girls. Boys. They turn. They tug. They grunt. They beat the place with jungle-limb clubs. Wallop it with rocks. Kick it. Pound the walls with their fists.

The more they can't get in, the more they want to.

Hence the word before *Hut: Forbidden*.

Some call it Don't Even Try.

"So what's your brilliant new idea?" says Ana Mae.

Jubilee grins. "We're always trying to bust in, right?"

"Yeah, so?"

"So how about this time"—she taps Ana Mae's chest with the red blade of the spade—"we bust *under*."

JACK

FEELING BETTER. It was just like old times with Kiki.
He can feel the day turning around, hope surging. He
heads for Tattooer.

In his own Newbie and Snotsipper days, Jack
thought Tattooer was *in* the building. Now he knows
better: Tattooer *is* the building. Or, to be more precise,
the robot. Its facade is the face of a clown. You walk up
three steps and climb into a nostril—left or right, it's
your choice. Some say that choice makes all the difference, whatever that means. It's a steep crawl up the
nose, like going the wrong way on a sliding board, but
you don't even think about it, you just do it.

Inside, two things happen. First your diaper is whipped off and catapulted through a hole in the roof. If you're standing outside, what you see is a stream of diapers popping out of the roof and flying in a great arc toward the far horizon. They never land, however, for at the height of the arc they burst into flame and glamorize the daytime sky like a parade of shooting stars.

The second thing that happens is you get your tattoo. Muddled memories recall a green misty light, a tickle on the belly, a smell like toasting marshmallows. Then, with a sound that's come to be known as "the turtle's toot," you're spit out the mouth. When you hit the ground, you announce yourself to Hokey Pokey: "I'm a kid!" More important, you're wearing your tattoo—and a pair of pants. You are now a Newbie. A Hokey Poker.

Standing at the end of the line of diaper-clad Newbie recruits, Jack has never felt more foolish. Fortunately there are only three ahead of him. He prays the line moves fast, before anyone sees him. It's bad enough that the Newbie in front of him looks up and says something that sounds like, "Ee foozanakka nugu."

When his turn comes, he quickly discovers he's got a problem: he can't fit up either nostril. So he enters via the mouth. Inside, true to his memory, a misty green light pervades, though it barely tints the gloom. Squinting, he makes out the Tickler, as it's called. He doesn't know what he must have thought of it the first time around. Now if he had to describe it, he might say *mechanical octopus*. It strikes him as surprising that at this point the Newbies don't run off screaming, for it's a little scary even to him. It's very low to the floor, no doubt to accommodate the height of its clients.

Jack drops to his knees and shuffles forward. He stops at what he hopes is the right spot. He pulls his shirt up. He's sweating. He waits. And waits. Nothing seems to be happening. The stubby, jointed mechanical arms seem to be locked in mid-gesture. Has he done something wrong? Can it tell he's not a Newbie? He crouches lower, sits on his heels. The dark light flickers. A sniff-like noise—twice—comes from somewhere. Now two of the arms are moving. They poke him gently on the stomach. Instantly they recoil and a red light is flashing and an alarm is wailing and something is happening beneath him and with a guttural gagging cough Tattooer barfs him backward and out of its mouth. He lands on his butt in the glaring daylight, at the feet of his Amigos.

AMIGOS

Dᴜꜱᴛʏ ᴀɴᴅ LᴀJᴏ ꜱᴛᴀʀᴇ ᴅᴜᴍʙʟʏ as Jack gets to his feet, dusts himself off. He doesn't look at them. He acts as if he doesn't know they're there. He walks off. He abruptly turns and comes back. He pulls up their shirts, first Dusty's, then LaJo's. He sags. He sighs.

"It's just me, isn't it? Nobody but me."

They nod.

"You knew?"

They nod.

"How long?"

Dusty clears his throat. "Just today. That's when we saw. This morning. LaJo saw it first, at the tracks."

Jack looks up, squints at the sundazzle. Their shadows are down to inches. "He'll be here soon," he says absently.

Dusty looks up, LaJo down. "Yeah," they say together.

Jack gazes off in the distance. "So what do you think?"

LaJo starts to say something, but Dusty cuts him off. "Nothin, Jack. It don't mean squat. It's just some . . . crazy thing. No sweat."

Jack looks at LaJo. LaJo doesn't want to speak, but Jack waits him out. LaJo shrugs. "Like he said, no sweat."

Jack keeps staring, repeats as if trying to memorize: "No sweat." He looks back at Tattooer. He grins feebly. "I figured it was worth a try."

Dusty, ever the tension-breaker, pokes Jack, laughs. "When you came shooting outta there . . . *backwards*—"

A flaming diaper vaults across the sky.

"What's it like in there?" says Dusty. "I forget."

"Creepy," says Jack.

They stare in silence as the diaper comet dissolves in a sooty puff. Dusty pokes LaJo. "Give it to him." LaJo doesn't move. Another poke, harder. "*Give* it."

LaJo turns. "No."

"Yes. He *needs* it. Give it."

LaJo's hands remain tightly in his pockets. "Some things you don't mess with."

"It ain't up to you. It's up to him."

They're speaking as if Jack isn't here.

Jack holds out his hand to LaJo. "Give."

LaJo stares at Jack.

"Give."

LaJo shrugs, gives.

It's a felt-tip marker. "I found it," says Dusty. "He snatched it."

Jack studies the marker. He removes the cap. The tip is black, well-worn. He hands it to Dusty, pulls up his shirt. A small, solitary smear remains on his stomach. Dusty kneels, hesitates, begins to draw. He pauses, looks up. "Tickle?"

"Nah," says Jack, but really it does.

Dusty goes back to work. LaJo sends them a sour look, turns away. A fresh Newbie pops from the maw of Tattooer: "I'm a kid!"

DESTROYER

THERE'S A POINT, when you're still far away, where the bluff looks like the end of the world. All you see is the top edge of the bluff and the sky, like someone took a knife and sliced Hokey Pokey off right there. Then, as you continue walking, you begin to see treetops beyond the bluff, and then the jungle and, through the trees, the creek, and then, when you reach the bluff's edge and look down, you see the tracks.

None of this catches Destroyer's attention. What he notices, emerging like a mirage from the heat-shimmer as he approaches, is a pair of girl bikes. They're parked by the blackberry bramble. One, an ordinary nag, is a purply color. The other one is special. It's yellow and glittery. Ribbons dangle from pink handlegrips. The saddle is fuzzy white. Fuzzy pink and white balls hang from the tail. Something is written on the flank. He knows exactly what he's looking at: the famous bike that the girl stole this morning. That used to be Scramjet. That used to be Jack's.

What's it doing here?

Where's the girl?

He wonders these things as he comes near.

JUBILEE

THERE'S ONLY ONE SPADE, so the girls take turns digging. At the moment it's Ana Mae. She's barely begun and already she's huffing. "I can't believe how hard this is."

"You don't have to believe," says Jubilee. "Just shut your mouth and do it."

"Why do little kids like to dig?" Ana Mae gasps. "What's fun about this?"

"I'm not answering your stupid questions," Jubilee growls. "Save your breath."

Ana Mae digs. Each stroke yields barely a handful

of coarse dirt and stones. Ana Mae is now grunting dramatically with every thrust of the red spade. She stops, bent, huffing. She steps back. She jabs the spade at the hole as she waits for her breath to return. "Look," she says.

Jubilee groans. "Look at what?"

"The hole."

"What about it?"

She jabs the blade at Jubilee. "First you dug. Then me. Then you. Then me. And look." She puts her arm in the hole. Her elbow still shows. "We'll *never* finish."

"Holy Harriet." Jubilee snatches the spade. "What a baby. Get outta the way." She sets to digging.

DESTROYER

KEEPS WAITING for a head to pop up, for someone to yell "Hey—you!" But it isn't happening. He's alone.

He stops ten feet away. He can't believe he's this close. He's almost afraid to stare directly at it. Scramjet. The legend. He knows that it knows he's here. He feels the energy streaming from it, as if flies are landing on his skin. Many times he has seen it streak across the land, the sprocket's silver whirl. He has heard the chain sing.

His thoughts go back to the last time he sat upon his beloved yellow Daffy Duck trike.

He takes a deep breath, takes one step forward . . .

JUBILEE

Dɪɢs . . . ᴅɪɢs . . .

DESTROYER

ARE YOU WAITING FOR ME? *Is that why you're here? Yellow, like Daffy? They broke my Daffy. Are you my prize because they broke my Daffy?*

JUBILEE

Cannot admit it to Ana Mae, but this digging is brutal. With every thrust, the blade thunks against stones. The bigger rocks she has to claw out with her hands. The hole is big enough now for her to put one foot in. The sun feels like it's close enough to touch. Her shirt is sticking to her skin. A pearl of sweat fattens on the end of her nose, falls. She'd give anything for a lemon-lime hokey pokey right now. Icy. Wet. Her shadow is a pencil line.

The blade clanks against a rock. She slumps. She needs a break. She's about to hand the spade over when

Ana Mae shrieks. She's staring at her hand with a look of horror. "I'm getting a *blister!*"

Jubilee goes back to work.

DESTROYER

STANDS BEFORE THE BIKE. He cannot read the word on the yellow flank. He assumes it is *Scramjet*. He can't believe he's this close. He reaches out, touches a pink handlegrip with the tip of his finger. Yes, it's real. He lays a hand lightly on the flank. He pets it. Nothing happens. The Great One is still, as if napping, beast and slim shadow leaning on the kickstand.

Do it.

I can't.

Do it.

It's not mine.

Who cares? Climb on. Ride. No one will know.

I might get hurt.

You might get the ride of your lifetime. You'll make history. They'll make a statue of you on Scramjet. Put it next to The Kid.

I'm scared.

You will amaze everyone. Now they'll be scared of you. Even Big Kids.

I'm little.

Not after you do it.

I can't.

They broke Daffy. Do it for Daffy.

I can't.

You are Destroyer of Worlds.

I can't reach the pedals.

The chain will sing to you.

I loved Daffy.

Do it!

JUBILEE

Focus . . . focus . . .

She tries not to think of her aching shoulders. She tries not to think of her wet armpits and dry mouth. She focuses on the prize. Soon they will know what's on the other side of the wall. She tries to picture it but finds that her thoughts dissolve like a lemon-lime hokey pokey on her tongue. No doubt it will be wonderful, but wonderful in what way? Will there be dazzle and spectacular things to see? Will it be the answer to a great mystery? Will it be wonderful in ways she cannot imagine? Is that the point? The prize? That the first person to enter Forbidden Hut will have an experience that cannot even be imagined by those left outside?

She digs . . . digs . . .

DESTROYER

"I am Destroyer of Worlds . . . I am Destroyer of Worlds . . . ," he whispers as he steps within the arc of the handlebar. And sees his problem at once: the saddle is too high—he needs a boost. And that's not going to happen, as he's alone out here on the bluff. The thought flitters in his brain: *Not that anybody would ever give me a boost.*

He looks about for something to step on—nothing but the berry thicket and a hole in the ground. Standing by the bike, the saddle head-high, he feels his littleness. Runt, the Daffy-killers called him. Well . . .

maybe for once runt is good. Maybe he doesn't need a boost. Maybe he doesn't even weigh enough to topple it over. Maybe he can just climb up onto this thing. Step on the pedal, step on the sprocket, lean into the top tube, swing a leg up and over. He'll do it on the kickstand side, and the kickstand will hold (*Please!*) because . . . *he's a runt.*

The kickstand's silver toe pierces the red dust. He's panting, as if he's just finished a race. He feels weak, shaky. He can't move.

Do it!

He curls his fingers around the top tube, loosely at first, now more firmly. He does not know whose pulse he's feeling, his or Scramjet's. With his right hand he grasps the back of the white fuzzy saddle. He lifts his left foot, places it gingerly upon the left-side pedal, waits . . . waits . . .

Do it!

He pushes himself off the ground until the pedal, the bike, the kickstand holds . . . holds . . . yes! Swings his right leg upward, catches the saddle on his knee-bend while shooting his right hand forward to the right grip, left hand to left grip, pulling, pulling up with his bent knee, pushing up with his hands . . . up . . . up . . .

and over! He's in the saddle! Aboard Scramjet! Harold Peter Bitterman Jr. tall in the saddle on Scramjet the Magnificent! His feet dangle freely, pedals far below. His arms are stretched to the limit, elbows locked. He leans into the grips. He dares whisper, "Let's go, boy."

And feels a shudder in the withers.

JUBILEE

"OH NO!"

Water comes gushing up from the bottom of the hole. Suddenly she's knee-deep in it. She wallops the Hut's wall with the spade. The red blade breaks off. "Crappo!" she yells, and pounds the broken handle upon the ground.

Ana Mae says, "Ace, shut up. Listen."

She follows Ana Mae's eyes back across the trees. "What?"

Ana Mae stands. "Hear that?"

At first there is only the soft, friendly chuckle of

the creek. Then, from the bluff, a scream. A little-kid scream.

Jubilee is up and out of the water hole. The little-kid scream is snipped, as if by scissors, by another sound, an inhuman sound, a sound they have never heard before and yet instinctively recognize.

Jubilee drops the handle. The girls gape at each other. "Hazel!"

They run.

DESTROYER

THE CHAIN IS NOT SINGING. The sound it makes cannot be described. It sets puppies and Newbies howling. Strangulated shrieks rise from deep in the loamy furrows of Doll Farm. Snugger pinkens. And Destroyer believes the sound is ripping him a third earhole between his eyes. He knows in this moment two things better than he has ever known anything:

1. He has made a *big* mistake.
2. It's too late to do anything about it.

The yellow beast is going so fast he feels his butt rising, his legs trailing in the wind. He is flat-out now, his stomach over the saddle, only his hands in touch with the bike. He is a superhero flying, swinging this way and that as the bike races past Stuff, nips the DON'T sign. Hippodrome, The Kid are blurs. Grass-sitters scatter at Cartoons. Destroyer sees Playground coming up, and now his stomach flops onto the saddle—Scramjet is slowing down. The indescribable noise becomes a whine, now a whispery whistle. The bike canters among the swings and comes to a stop. Destroyer is draped over the saddle, fingers frozen around the grips, too terrified to move. Suddenly the bike rears on its hind wheel and deposits him onto the ground as neatly as a truck-dumped load.

JACK

Hɪs ʜᴇᴀʀᴛ ʟᴇᴀᴘs!

Scramjet is coming toward them and it's not the girl aboard. It's a little kid, flying flat-out Superman-style from the handlegrips. Scramjet is making a noise that would split the moon, but it's music to Jack's ears.

He stands stunned with his Amigos as Superkid and Scramjet go by in a flash of yellow, two legs and a string of pom-poms.

"It's that little runt creep," Dusty shouts over the noise.

They watch as Scramjet barrels, veers, tilts, gallops

through Hokey Pokey, sometimes losing sight except for the yellow cloud of dust. Jack wonders how in the world the kid got the bike from the girl, but he's too happy to wonder for long. When they see the bike finally slowing down in Playground, they head over there. They laugh as the bike rears and dumps the runt.

A crowd has already gathered. It parts as Jack and his boys come through to backslaps and hearty greetings: "Hey, Jack! . . . Hey, Jack!" Scramjet appears to be at rest, but Jack knows better. He feels the energy coming off the violated flanks. He knows if he touches the tires, they will be hot and hard as rock and pulsing. He knows you can take the bike out of the herd but you can't take the herd out of the bike. He knows his highstrung steed, after a fast ride, needs no one and no thing, and that's why it stands straight though the kickstand is up.

Dusty bestrides the dumped kid. "Runt," he sneers. "Wha'd you *think* would happen?"

"Lay off," says LaJo, a rare lilt in his voice. "He did us a favor. Give him a medal."

The runt, his terror thawing like a hokey pokey at high noon, begins to shake and sob and crawls away on hands and knees. A boyvoice calls: "It's yours, Jack! Take it back!"

Someone else picks up the call—"Take it back, Jack!"—and now there's a chant of mobbed boyvoices:

"TAKE IT BACK, JACK!"

"TAKE IT BACK, JACK!"

"TAKE IT BACK, JACK!"

Jack trades a look with his Amigos, grins: as if he had anything else in mind. Dusty and LaJo back off, respecting Jack's moment.

Jack approaches his bike. He's torn between laughing (for joy) and crying (at the paint job, which, he can see up close now, is sloppy, as if done by a Snotsipper). Joy wins, but he keeps the laugh inside.

For starters, he rips off the pom-pom tail and pink ribbons. The mob cheers. The rest of the atrocities—the pink grips, the saddle fuzz, the paint job, the name—can wait. He leans into the bar, whispers "Scramjet," and believes he hears it whisperwhinny back: "Jack." He mounts. Feels all the tension of the morning drain out of him. Thinks: *I'm home*. His swallow double-clutches. Until today he had not known he could be so emotional. No pedal push is needed—Scramjet moves. The mob parts in reverent silence. There is only the soft crunch of tire rolling over ground and the distant tootle of Hippodrome.

He guides Scramjet out of Playground. He is in no

hurry. There will be time for fast. For now he is content to canter, to gratefully reclaim his bike, his world, himself. Jailhouse . . . Tattooer . . . Cartoons . . . on they roll. With every passing Hokey Pokey feature, he recovers another piece of his life. Trucks . . . Tantrums . . . Everywhere kids stop what they're doing and watch. The occasional Snotsipper or Sillynilly blurts "Hey, Jack!" while the oldest kids, shocked at the pairing of girl bike and boy rider, stand mutely and wonder uneasily about themselves.

Beyond Tantrums, Mitchell now appears to have uncovered all the petrified remains of the fossil megabike. Bikasaurus, Mitchell is calling it. He's got the frame together and is trying to fit a wheel. A couple of Snotsippers sit on their haunches nearby, rapt.

They roll on toward The Kid. They pass beneath the great stone arm: it seems a blessing. He sees Gorilla Hill in the distance. He hears again the girl's demonic scream, as surely embedded in his brain as any fossil in the ground. He knows the only way to disinter that scream is to cancel it with a downhill ride of his own. He's about to rein toward the Hill when Scramjet veers sharply to the right. Must have gone over a stone. Jack tugs on the left grip and a funny thing happens: nothing. The handlebar doesn't move; the front wheel maintains its course. Jack tugs harder—again, nothing. Jack looks down. Chain, sprocket, steering column—all seem in order.

This time Jack tugs with both hands, wrenches hard, actually, but the bike stubbornly refuses to budge. He leans in the saddle, whispers, "Hey, boy, what's up?" *That girl*, he thinks. She's done something to his bike, bunged it up somehow, and now it won't turn.

Just for the heck of it, Jack presses on the pedal. Nothing happens. He presses hard. Tromps. The bike keeps its steady, unhurried pace. It seems to be heading for the bluff. Alarm comes as a quick nip between the shoulders. He squeezes the brakes—nothing. And suddenly knows: *I'm not driving it—it's driving me.*

Once again he feels the day falling apart. Dreading yet unable to stop himself, he pulls up his shirt and dares to look: Dusty's felt-tip tattoo has already faded to a faint gray smear. An enormous sadness comes over him. His mouth feels furry. In the shimmering, shadowless distance he sees two figures running his way. . . .

JUBILEE

Ana Mae is first to see. "Look!"

They stop.

Jubilee squints under her cap brim. "You think?"

"Yeah. It's him."

"What's he doing?"

"He's coming this way."

"I can see that, dummy. *Why?*"

They stand in the dust. Bike and rider are coming slowly.

"Maybe he doesn't know it's you," says Ana Mae.

"Maybe he does," says Jubilee. "I should've brought that shovel."

"He's alone," says Ana Mae. "We're two."

There seems nothing else to do, nowhere else to go. They stand, wait, wait.

Slowly bike and rider emerge from the heatshimmer. "He's not pedaling," Jubilee says.

Now they hear the soft tire crunch. Now they see his face. Jubilee is surprised. It is not the face she expected. Her fisted fingers uncurl.

The bike stops directly in front of her. The boy seems in shock, as if he's just awakened in a strange place. He does not look at her. She sees that the handlegrip ribbons and the pom-pom tail are gone. Otherwise, Hazel looks the same. It occurs to Jubilee that the boy and bike might stay there all day. All she knows for sure is that the next move is not hers. At last the boy drops a foot to the ground, swings the other leg over, dismounts. He looks at her now. All she sees in his eyes is sadness, a sadness as big as the sky. He does not put the kickstand down; he simply releases the bike. As it falls, she instinctively reaches out, catches it by a grip. When she looks up, he's walking away, and in the distance she hears the familiar *wooguh! wooguh!* of the red rubber cart horn and the excited cries that fly across Hokey Pokey every day at high noon: "He's here! . . . He's here!"

HOKEY POKEY MAN

IN THE SKY the sun has stopped directly over The Kid. In all of Hokey Pokey only The Kid's arm casts a shadow.

The Hokey Pokey Man gives the red rubber bladder another squeeze: *wooguh! wooguh!* Kids are running from all directions, many already shouting:

"Cherry!"

"Root beer!"

"Black cherry!"

"Grape!"

The Hokey Pokey Man mops his brow with a large andkerchief, stuffs it back in the bib pocket of his white overalls. A white stubble of whiskers covers his face. A bright green beret tops his head.

A great block of ice sits in the bed of the white hand-pushed cart. It is flanked on three sides by all the colors of the world: bottled syrup in every flavor a kid could desire. With a flourish he sweeps a striped towel from the ice, jerks the scraper from its well and gruffs, "First up."

A boy Snotsipper steps up, barks "Orange." Immediately the Hokey Pokey Man sets to work. Leaning forward, with a grunt that is more form than necessity, he pushes the scraper three times along the length of the ice block, which gleams in the sun like a diamond. The teeth that shave the ice feed slush into the square metal bowl. The left hand plucks a white cone-shaped paper cup from a tall stack. A tap to settle the slush, the bowl hatch swings open and deposited into the cup is a perfectly square snowball—a hokey pokey. The right hand returns the scraper to the well, reaches for the orange bottle of syrup. A multitude of eyes gawk as the upturned bottle delivers one . . . two . . . three . . . four . . . five squirts—and long squirts they are—into the slush, blushing it into such pure essence that it virtually cries out: *Orange!*

The Snotsipper is speechless, entranced. The hokey

pokey floats before his eyes until someone jabs him. He comes to his senses, snatches it and walks off. A mob of tongues salivate at the sound of his teeth sinking into sweet ice.

"Grape," says the next in line.

All is orderly. There is little noise, no fooling around. A sense that nonsense will not be tolerated pervades the crowd. Kids who a minute ago were squalling and brawling now stand quietly in line, awaiting their turn.

"Chocolate."

"Watermelon."

"Strawberry."

Occasionally one of the youngest will say, "Do you have such-and-such?" The Hokey Pokey Man does not answer. He simply reaches for the bottle of such-and-such. There is no flavor he does not have.

"Licorice."

"Bubble gum."

"Jalapeño."

Now and then a "Please" or "Thank you" is heard. Most say nothing. With older kids it simply is what it always is: high noon and the Hokey Pokey Man. Should they thank the sky for being blue? Younger ones are struck speechless by the dazzle of the Man's hands, the rainbow of syrup bottles, the castaneting clack of the ice scraper. By the time they reach the head of the line, they are too famished for words, too grateful for manners.

The population is served quickly. As the last of the patrons walk off, the Hokey Pokey Man mops his brow and pulls the towel over the great block of ice. The sun moves. From objects and bodies everywhere shadows begin to seep.

JACK

PAPER CUPS LITTER THE LANDSCAPE, bleed flavors, darken the dust.

Jack walks.

He is empty.

When Scramjet went to the girl, a plug was pulled and everything inside him poured out. He is nothing but skin and a name. Maybe not even that. He wants to say it aloud—*Jack!*—to confirm his existence, but he cannot summon the strength to do so. He doesn't bother to lift his shirt and check Dusty's tattoo. He knows it's gone.

He would call his Amigos, but there is only empty air where his Tarzan yell used to be.

Something is over. Something is finished. He knows this now. Whatever it is, it's more than a tattoo, more than a bike. An incredible thought comes to him as he drags across the barren landscape. He has just suffered the greatest tragedy of his life. He has lost his beloved bike, his Scramjet, and to a girl—to *the* girl—no less. But even that is not the incredible thought. The incredible thought is this: *I don't even care.*

At first, in the distance, it is merely a wrinkle in the heatshimmer, but it soon becomes the Hokey Pokey Man pushing his cart, going wherever it is he goes each day, one more element of Jack's life draining away. The wheels of the cart waver in the shimmer. *No more hokey pokeys for me*, Jack thinks as he plods on, and so, when he looks up again, is surprised to find the distance shrinking. He can now hear the tinkle of the bottles, the crunch of the cart's wheels. The Hokey Pokey Man has stopped. He seems to be waiting. He throws the towel off the block of ice, grabs the scraper. Jack looks around, sees no one else. Hears a voice, crusty: "Time's flyin, Mr. Boy."

Was that him? Did he speak? To me?

As Jack approaches, he sees the Hokey Pokey Man has already set to work. He dumps the hokey pokey into a cup, drenches it with generous slugs of Jack's usual—root beer. As he hands Jack the square snowball, he does something he's never done before: he looks at Jack. The stubbled face is as stony as ever, like The Kid's, and yet somehow Jack feels himself washed over by something he can only perceive as a smile. The look lasts but a moment, and already the Hokey Pokey Man is slinging the towel over the ice and pushing off. Jack watches. He is mesmerized by the crunch and tinkle of the cart—a music he has never heard before—and now the unexpected, crusty voice: "Sayonara, kid." And now, from somewhere beyond the sun, the whistle of a train.

AMIGOS

Dusty is stomping about, decapitating dandelion puffballs. When he spots a new one, he stomps over to it and kicks, sending fuzz flying. All the while muttering: "What's goin on? . . . What's goin on?" He no longer addresses himself to LaJo. He seeks answers from the great blue cosmos above, the ground below, the dandelions, as if kicking them will knock answers loose. His flung-off cap lies in the dust.

From afar they watched in stunned disbelief as Jack rode his violated Scramjet right up to the girl, handed it over to her and walked away. Dusty has been ranting ever since.

"Your nose is running," says LaJo, who takes a seat on a home-plate-size rock.

Dusty wipes his nose with his shirtsleeve. Stomps, kicks. "Where did his tattoo go? . . . Why's he acting like this? . . . Is this some kinda nightmare we're in? . . . Is somebody playin a trick on us?" He faces the faceless sky, bellows: "*Huh?*"

The sky does not reply, but LaJo does. "If you shut up for a minute, I'll tell you."

Dusty, who breathes befuddlement like others breathe air, has not really been expecting an answer to his questions, so he is surprised at LaJo's remark. He is constantly surprised to find that LaJo seems to know more about life than he does. He turns, waits.

LaJo keeps him waiting. He often does this. LaJo picks up a pebble and tosses it idly. He spots a dandelion fuzzball. He rears back, honks and—*pthoo!*—fires a hocker. Misses. At last he says, "He's leaving." This is another thing LaJo does. His answers, when they finally come, are too short.

Dusty's jaw drops, eyes bulge. He waits. Waits for more. When he realizes nothing more is coming, he screeches: "*Huh? . . . What? . . .* Waddaya mean *leaving? . . .* What's *that* s'pose to mean?"

LaJo shrugs. "Leaving. Away. Gone. Vamoosed."

Dusty stands there gaping, blinking.

A Newbie comes running, yelling, "LaJo!" It's the red-haired runt LaJo got stuck with at Tattooer. The Newbie crashes into LaJo. "LaJo! C'mon! Let's play! C'mon!" The kid is pulling so hard on LaJo's hand his tiny butt is scraping the ground.

LaJo glances down, looks away. "No."

The kid yammers on. "C'mon, LaJo! Play with me! Play! Play! Play!"

LaJo leans down. The kid stops pulling. He thinks LaJo is going to play. LaJo bends until his face is one inch from the kid's. LaJo bellows: "Beat it!"

The force of LaJo's voice knocks the runt onto his butt. His eyes are round as bike wheels. He gets up. He kicks LaJo in the shin and runs off. He does not cry.

The incident with the Newbie has barely dented Dusty's brain. He stares at LaJo. He shakes his head with vigor. "No," he says.

LaJo's eyebrows arch. "No?"

"No."

"No what?"

"Jack ain't gone nowhere."

LaJo shrugs. "Fine. He ain't going nowhere."

Dusty kicks more dandelions. He wheels. "So *where*, huh? *Where's* he going?"

LaJo shrugs. "How should I know?"

Dusty turns, arms outstretched. "Where is there to go *to*? . . . This is it. . . . Where else *is* there?" He points to the sky. "The moon? Is that where he's going? The moon?" LaJo is picking dirt from his fingernails. Dusty jutjaws. "So how do *you* know all this anyway? Huh? How do you know he's going away?"

"I didn't say *know*. You did. I just think it. It reminds me of something."

"Reminds you? What's it remind you of?"

LaJo lets out a long breath. "The Story."

Dusty picks his cap up from the dust. He takes special care replacing it. He is vaguely pleased to find, on this crazy day, that his head remains atop his neck. "Story? What story?"

LaJo snorts, doesn't bother to answer. It's a dumb question, as even Dusty knows. Because there is only one story. The one that comes out of the walnut shells. Sometime before the end of the first day, every Newbie discovers more than a tattoo on his or her stomach. It's pockets. Pants with pockets. And in the right front pocket of every pair of pants is half a walnut shell.

There are no instructions. There is only eternal instinct, two voiceless commands:

Never throw away your shell.

At bedtime hold it to your ear.

When they do, they hear The Story.

THE STORY

IT IS A TALE OF HOKEY POKEY. Of The Kid. Of The Kid's early days as a Newbie and a crybaby Snotsipper and his adventurous growth into a lisping Gappergum, an endlessly laughing Sillynilly, a Longspitter, a Groundhog Chaser and, finally, a Big Kid. By this time The Kid, like most Big Kids, no longer listened to The Story at night. But, as The Story goes, *he carried his walnut shell everywhere he went.*

Little kids never tire of The Story. Every night they hear it for the first time. Every night they are both horrified and thrilled by the ending. For in the end The Kid announces: *I am going away.*

The Hokey Pokers in The Story do not understand. *Away to where?* they say. *To Great Plains? The Mountains?*

Away from Hokey Pokey, The Kid says.

They laugh. *No way!*

Tomorrow I will be gone, he says.

Tomorrow? they say. *What's tomorrow?*

There is no answer. There is only a growing dread, a conviction that something must be done. For they love The Kid—from Newbies to Big Kids. They don't want him to go. When The Kid is the caller, boys and girls dance the hokey pokey together:

> *You put your right foot in,*
> *You put your right foot out;*
> *You put your right foot in,*
> *And you shake it all about.*
> *You do the hokey pokey,*
> *And you turn yourself around.*
> *That's what it's all about!*

And then The Kid says, *You will forget me.*

That does it.

So they trick him. They lure him out to Thousand Puddles, to stomp and splash. *One last time,* they say.

They tell him to lie down on the ground, they have a surprise for him. And then they attack him with tickles. No one, not even The Kid, can withstand a mass tickle attack. His laughter blows the fuzz off dandelions a half-mile away. But more important, he is helpless—and the attack goes into its second stage: mud. As The Kid helplessly howls, they cover him in puddle mud. They don't stop until every inch of him is slathered in a thick coat of sludge. They back off and watch the mud dry and then harden in the sun. It happens quickly. They touch it. It's like stone. The Kid, on his back, is pointing straight up at the sky. They haul him to an open spot between Tantrums and Hippodrome, a bare, dusty mini-desert inhabited only by hot-rodding trikers. They prop him up—and there he is today. The Kid. Pointing to who knows where. Some say he's pointing to Forbidden Hut. Some say he's the only one who knows how to get in. But now he's not going anywhere.

Though little kids are horrified at the way The Story ends, at the same time they love it. It satisfies something deep inside them. If they had to use a word, they might say *delicious*. But in fact it sweetens them beyond the belly, beyond the reach even of the Hokey Pokey Man.

Big Kids know something little kids do not: The Story ends not with a period, but with a question mark. It's as if there's an ending beyond the ending, a suspicion that there's more to The Story than the walnut shell is telling. The older you get, the closer you feel to the real ending—but you never quite get there. And so rumors fill in the blanks:

The walnut shell does finish The Story, but only after the listener falls asleep.

If you give the statue of The Kid a good whack, it will crack open and reveal a still-beating heart.

Under cover of darkness The Kid's ghost oozes out of the statue and catches a ghost train out of Hokey Pokey.

The voice in the walnut shell belongs to your sleep monster.

Rumors and questions: kids suck the juice from them like syrup from a soaked hokey pokey. They fall asleep, some in favorite spots, some where they drop, shell in hand. Curiously, there is one question no one ever thinks to ask: How is it that when you wake up every morning, the walnut shell is back in your pocket?

AMIGOS

DUSTY LAUGHS, screeches. "It's a *story*! It's a *fairy tale*!"

LaJo shrugs. "Is it?"

Dusty is speechless. He looks around. There are no fuzzballs left to kick. "So what are you saying? Jack's gonna turn into a *statue*?"

With his finger LaJo traces the letter *J* in the dust. "'One day when he woke up things were different.'"

Dusty screeches. "*Huh?*"

LaJo traces an A in the dust. "You heard me."

Dusty did hear, and now, as he stares at LaJo, he remembers. He's heard the words before, hundreds of times. He may no longer listen carefully to his shell every night, but like every other Hokey Poker, he can recite The Story word for word. And there they are, at the start of The Kid's last day: *One day when he woke up things were different.*

"So?" says Dusty.

LaJo ticks them off on his fingers. "So. Bike gone. Tattoo gone. Him crying. What we just saw with him and the girl. Different."

Dusty swells defiantly. "Jack ain't a story. Jack is Jack."

LaJo traces a C in the dust. "'Big Boy was gone.'"
Big Boy was gone too.

Big Boy: The Kid's bike. As precious to him as Scramjet was to Jack.

Dusty gapes, blinks, gushes half a laughball. "Aw, c'mon, man . . . that don't mean—"

"'The Kid was not himself.'"

It's right there, in The Story. For the first time in his life it strikes Dusty that these are the most chilling words of all: *The Kid was not himself.*

He watches LaJo trace the final letter in the dust: K. Dusty feels his heart borne off on an irresistible zephyr as he whispers the name of his friend, his Amigo—"Jack"—and from the far horizon of his soul, his heart calls back: . . . *is not himself.*

JACK

Is there wind in a whistle?

Jack feels himself nudged along like tumbleweed across the dusty flats of Hokey Pokey. Until today Jack has steered his own way through this life. Each day has been a parade of decisions. *Now I'll saddle up and go riding with my Amigos. Now I'll give Kiki a baseball lesson. Now I'll skip stones across the creek.* Suddenly, today, *now* is out of his hands. He's at the mercy of some unseen force blowing him from moment to moment. He no longer *goes* to a place; he simply, helplessly, *finds himself* there. Tumbleweed.

Behind him he hears the familiar tick and whir of Scramjet's wheels. Then her voice: "Hey, Jacko! Jacko!" He keeps walking. There are things he must do, though he's not sure what. She circles him, leaning, carving tracks in the dust, squawking: "Jacko! Jacko!" He plods on. She circles, circles, closer with each pass. Each time she passes before him, he notices the ponytail flying from the hole in the back of her baseball cap. This is not new. He's noticed it before. And the yellow ribbon that bunches her toasted honeywheat hair as it streams from the cap—that's not new either. What's new is his eyes—he can't take them off the ribbon. They see how it's bowed like a shoelace. But not like a shoelace too, because the ribbon is so wide. He didn't know ribbon could be so wide, so . . . *ribbony*. And yellow! He's seen bananas and he's seen lemons, but he doesn't think he's ever seen yellow as yellow as the yellow of that ribbon. It's like the sun painted itself into a knot around her streaming hair. These new eyes of his, so used to watching the flight of a ball, now follow the fluttering tails of the golden bow.

Now, passing closer than ever, she reaches out and clips his cap—"Jacko!"—and it spins to the ground. He stops, picks it up, resumes his trek. She pulls up ten feet away, directly in his path, her eyes flashing, her grin wicked, waiting, daring, mocking, her foot on the pedal, poised to bolt. She passes from his sight as he detours around her. He feels a thump between his shoulder blades. "Chick-*ken*! Ba-*bawlllk*! Ba-*bawlllk*!" He walks on. Silence behind him. He discovers that his face is smiling.

JUBILEE

ANA MAE, who has been watching from a distance, rides up. "What happened?"

Jubilee's puzzled eyes follow the retreating boy. "I don't know."

"What did he say?"

"Nothing."

"Not even when you knocked his cap off?"

"Nope."

"Didn't even call you a name? He always calls you names."

Jubilee shakes her head.

Ana Mae looks upward, giggles with fond remembrance. "The way he calls you *girl*? Makes it sound like a badword."

"Not this time."

Ana Mae fingerjabs. "At least he gave you a dirty look, right? Or spit at you? Remember that one time?"

Jubilee shakes her head. "Nuh. Thing."

Ana Mae joins her friend staring after the boy. Her voice, even as it speaks, gropes for a handhold. "You took his bike. Ace . . . you *took his bike*."

"Not really *took*," says Jubilee. Time to tell the truth. "I woke up this morning and it was just"—she shakes her head, still not believing—"*there*."

Ana Mae thinks on it, throws up her hands. "OK, fine, it was *there*. But you didn't exactly give it *back*, did you?" She pokes Jubilee. "*Did* you?"

Jubilee's stare is no longer puzzled, just empty. "No."

Ana Mae walks her bike off a ways, stands and stares, loops back. She lightly bumps her front tire into Jubilee's. "Ace?"

Jubilee is staring beyond the boy now, to the way things were. "Huh?" she says absently.

"Maybe he doesn't hate you anymore."

Jubilee does not seem to have heard. She blinks, turns to Ana Mae, stares, turns away, says nothing.

Ana Mae follows Jubilee's gaze to the horizon. Thunder rumbles beyond the Mountains. Panic lays a cold finger on the back of her neck. "Jubilee? . . . Ace? . . ." She smooths out the shake in her voice. "*You* still hate *him*"—she swallows—"don't you?"

She waits one eternity. Two. No answer. "Ace, you're creeping me out. You still hate him, don't you?"

The distant tootle of Hippodrome tints the silence. At last Jubilee's lips slide into their famously wicked grin. "He's a boy, ain't he?"

KIKI

JACK IS SCARED. He doesn't know what of.

Jack is thrilled. He doesn't know why.

He tumbles on. He drains the last of his root beer hokey pokey. He crumples the paper cone.

He is here and he must do things but he doesn't know what. He is here and he is going somewhere but he doesn't know where.

Sayonara, kid.

He doesn't know what and he doesn't know where and he doesn't know why, but that's OK because he doesn't need to know, just move, move. The force he has felt behind him now seems within, driving him: a second, tumbledown heart.

Kids call. "Hey, Jack! . . . Hey, Jack!"

He waves.

Tumbles.

Comes to Kiki.

Kiki is at The Wall. The Wall, about five spits long and a spit high, is made of brick. It is for bouncing things off of (tennis balls, soccer balls, junked tires, tin cans, dolls' heads) or crashing things into (trucks, model airplanes, jawbreakers, cantaloupes, cantaloupe-filled wagons). Today, like most days, Kiki is bouncing a moldy green tennis ball off The Wall, catching it with his cheap scrap of a fielder's glove. As soon as he spots Jack, he drops the tennis ball, grabs his black-taped baseball, tosses it. "Hey, Jack!"

Jack is already pulling Mr. Shortstop from his belt. They move away from The Wall. They take their positions, fall silently into the routine. The kid readies himself: tilted forward, balanced, fingers spread and twitching, ready for anything. Jack goes through the progression: ground balls, pop flies. And finally into the long windup for the skyscraper—and suddenly, not even thinking about it, Jack finds his right arm snapping a surprise ground ball at the kid. Only this time it's no ordinary grounder. It's an evil, hissing dust ripper that catches the kid totally off guard, caroms off the heel of his mitt, slams into his shoulder and skitters away.

The kid drops his glove, grabs his shoulder, squeals in pain. He looks at Jack, eyes brimming, lip trembling. Clearly he expects something from Jack: a comforting word, a gentle hand, an explanation. But all he gets is a single, dry question: "Surprised?"

The kid doesn't trust his voice. He sniffles, nods.

"Why surprised?" Jack's voice is calm, steady. "You're supposed to be ready for anything, right? Didn't I tell you a thousand times to be ready for anything?"

The kid nods, kneads his shoulder, winces.

"So you weren't ready for anything, were you?"

The kid shakes his head.

"OK. So what's the next thing you did wrong?"

The kid bleats: "I missed it."

Jack smiles. "Wrong."

Confusion piles onto shock and hurt. "Wrong?"

Jack wags his head. "You're allowed to miss. Did I ever tell you you're not allowed to miss?"

The kid thinks about it. He's wondering if this is a trick question. His answer sounds like a question: "No?"

"No. Right. Nobody's perfect. So, let's try again—what did you do wrong?"

The kid is feeling better now. But he's still stumped. "I don't know."

"I'll give you a hint," says Jack. "You're still doing it."

The kid is flummoxed. He's ready to cry again.

"OK," says Jack, taking pity, "look around you." The kid looks around. "What do you see?"

He sees weeds and scraggly bushes and of course The Wall, but he knows none of these is the answer. Now he sees it. "The ball?" It's sitting in the dust a spit and a half away.

Jack nods. "The ball. Right. And what's it doing over there?"

The kid blinks, gropes. "I missed it?"

Jack nods. "You missed it. And what did you do after you missed it?"

Another tricky question. "Uh . . . nothing?"

"You *gave up*!" Jack says it so sharply the kid jumps. "You missed it and the ball rolled over there and you did not go running after it . . . did you?"

"No."

"No. You gave up. You stood there like a big baby

looking at your empty glove and crying like a baby—
Oh boo-hoo boo-hoo I missed it—and while you're feeling all sorry for your baby self because the big bad baseball didn't bounce like you thought it would, the ball's sitting over there in the dirt and the other team's players are circling the bases and your team is now losing. Why? Because . . . *You. Gave. Up.*"

Jack wonders if he's gone too far. Maybe. But these things need to be said—now.

The kid's lip is trembling. He stares at Jack, silently pleading for more words, softer words. But Jack looks away. It's in the kid's hands now. In his heart. Suddenly the kid darts for the ball, snatches it, fires him a strike.

Jack rolls the dusty black-taped ball in his fingers. "So, let's try again. What did you do wrong?"

"I didn't chase it." The kid's voice is steady.

"You just stood there going *boo-hoo*. You gave up."

The kid barks: "I gave up!"

"You quit."

"I quit!"

"From now on, when you make a mistake, you're gonna chase the ball down—right? You're gonna clean up your mess and not be a big *boo-hoo* baby—right?"

"Right!"

Jack cups his ear. "What?"

"*Right!*"

Jack whips another grounder at the kid, harder even than the last. It takes a bad hop and bounces off the kid's chest, but this time the kid scrambles after it, plucks it, fires it back, the ball shedding yellow dust. He peppers the kid with more hard ones. He knows the kid won't catch them. Heck, Jack himself probably couldn't catch them. The kid is scared. Who wouldn't be, ball coming at you that fast, badhopping off stones? But that's not the thing. The thing is, the kid hangs in there. Frog-eyed terrified as he is of taking one in the chops, he holds his ground, he chases down every miss. No quitting. No *boo-hoo*ing.

Finally he rewards the kid with the skyscraper. The moment he slings it into the air, he knows it's different from all the others. It rises majestically into the blue, arcing toward the sun. The kid just stands there gaping, glove at his side, as the ball dwindles to the size of a peppercorn before vanishing, a pupil in the golden eye that looks down on Hokey Pokey's days. The kid shades his eyes, squints, readies himself for the catch. A posse of Snotsippers on trikes has stopped, gaping upward, scanning the sky for the ball, the ball that is not coming down. Jack wonders, *What's going on?* But not for long, for he senses that whatever is going on, it's just another strange thing in this strangest of all days.

He's done now. He's said the words to the kid, all of them. There's only one thing left to do. He gazes fondly at the glove that cradles his left hand. He smells for one last time the sweet oiled leather. He kisses it. Gently he slips the disgraceful rag from the kid's dangling hand. The kid, staring skyward in stupefied wonder, never notices. Jack slips Mr. Shortstop onto the kid's hand, gives the kid a light rumptap and moves on.

JACK

FEELS GOOD. Maybe better than good. Maybe even the best ever. But he doesn't know why—and now suddenly he does. It's movement. The sheer, raw exhilaration of *movement*. Movement unlike any he's ever experienced. Not the familiar movement of his own legs, or Scramjet's spinning wheels. It's more. The force that seemed inside him a few minutes ago now seems to be outside him again, beneath him, a current carrying him down some unseen stream, a current that's moving faster and faster, toward . . . *what?*

He looks back. The crowd of little kids is growing,

twenty, thirty upturned faces, searching the sky, poised, mitts twitching, waiting for the ball that is not coming down.

And now here she comes again. The girl, shucking dust over the flats, aiming straight at him. He takes his cap off—at least deny her that. She circles him as she did before, cutting a rolling hoop in the dust as he continues to walk. But this time she says nothing. No squawking. No insults. Just the soft crinkle of Scramjet's tires.

He wonders if she's trying to provoke him, daring him to reach out, start something. He remembers when they first met, both of them Snotsippers. She crashed her trike into his, not far from the DON'T sign, knocked both of them off their seats. It was an accident—to this day he's still sure of that—but for her it quickly became something else. As he picked himself up and stood there mooning over his dented trike, debating whether to cry or not, she climbed into the saddle, backed up, and rammed his trike again. And—as he gaped like a moronic cow—again! She was a shark. A lion. She had just gotten a taste of human blood—in particular, *his* blood—and now there was no stopping her.

Even at that age Jack knew he had two choices: run

away bawling or strike back. He struck back. He climbed onto his trike, and the two of them had their own little demolition derby. Half of Hokey Pokey came to hoot and cheer. In the end both trikes were wrecked, left in the dust, mangled wheels retching one last turn like the final flip of a dying lizard's tail. Jack and the girl both swaggered into the howling mob, pumping arms, claiming victory.

That was the beginning, the start of a war without a cease-fire. Oh they had their bikes and their high-noon hokey pokeys and their friends—but as much as anything, they had each other. Every morning Jack awoke knowing *she* was somewhere out there, ready to trade him hate for hate, mock for mock. They might appear to others to ignore each other, but in fact, Jack knew, each was always acutely aware of the other, as the wary eyes of the antelope track the jackal.

Of course, sometimes the attention they gave each other got loud and trashy:

"Outta my way, germ!"

"Donkey lips!"

"Poopnose!"

"You're so ugly your face is jealous of your butt!"

"You smell so bad the flies won't even land on you!"

"Watermelonhead!"

"Pimplebrain!"

"Boy!"

"Girl!"

In a way that Jack cannot articulate, he knows that she has shaped his life, given him something to grow against. Out of habit he tries to ignore her as she circles him. He turns his focus inward, for something truly remarkable seems to be happening. The seething burn she has always ignited inside him—it's gone. He feels nothing but a kind of humming, foamy peacefulness. He wonders how long he's been smiling. And finally he has to sneak a peek, then another, because he just can't get enough of that flying yellow ribbon.

He walks on, and the words leap from his mouth: "Remember when we busted up our trikes?"

She's circling behind him as he says it. He can hear her pull to a stop. He wonders if she heard him. He wonders why he said it. He keeps walking.

ANA MAE

NOW THAT SHE THINKS ABOUT IT, she honestly cannot remember ever speaking to a boy, except of course things like "Takes one to know one" and "Don't even think about it, dirtball." Certainly she has never had a conversation with one and until this moment doubted she ever would. But here she is, thanks to the lunacy of this day, compelled in the direction of the enemy—the Amigos, as they absurdly call themselves. Two-thirds of them anyway. Maybe they can tell her what's going on. Obviously their pal the Jack boy has been chewing on locoweed or something—anybody can see that. And

Ana Mae couldn't care less. What she does care about is the effect on Jubilee. The Jack boy seems to have acquired some sort of weird gravity, and it's pulling her best friend into its orbit.

They're looking at her as she pedals toward them. They can't believe it. She can see it in their eyes. She can't believe it either. She hates this. She's terrified. What if they gang up on her? She repeats to herself: "Only for Ace . . . only for Ace . . ."

She almost has to laugh. If she didn't know better, she might think they were harmless, sitting there all innocent-looking, as if they're not even boys, as if they're not responsible for everything wrong in the world. Even their bikes are a mess, dented nags flopped akimbo in the dirt. The brown boy, LaJo, thinks he's so cool. Shrugs a lot. Never smiles. Never surprised. That's what she hates most about him, that he's never surprised. She hit him in the back of the head with a water balloon once and all he did was slowly turn and look at her. Thing was, he didn't stop looking. She wanted to scream *Do something!* but all he did was stare—a lazy, stupid stare, no less—so finally she just stuck her tongue out and took off. This was when they were little.

And the other one. Dusty. Can't stand him for opposite reasons. Never shuts up. Whines and giggles like a Sillynilly. Tags after the Jack boy like a puppy. Still cries. Sneaks off to Snuggle Stop. He stands, his eyes getting wider and wider as she approaches, while the LaJo kid, squatting on a rock, looks lazily away, pretending she's not here. As she brakes her bike, she decides the best way is to just plunge: "So what are you wingnuts doing to Jubilee?"

That gets LaJo's attention. He doesn't turn to her but his head actually cranks up a notch. Meanwhile, the Dusty boy responds brilliantly: "Huh?"

"Is this bike thing some kinda trick you're playing on Jubilee? Some kinda joke?"

Dustymusty stupidly stares, blinks. If he says *Huh?* again, she's gonna run him over—and suddenly hears herself say it, snapping at the crybaby: "*Huh?*"

When the answer finally comes, it's from the other direction, the cool one: "It's no joke."

Glory be—it speaks! She continues to face the Dusty crybaby. "Really? How so? What's going on?"

Something new comes into the Dusty one's eyes. Something frightened. "It ain't her," he says. "It ain't us." His voice is wavering. "It's him."

She's beginning to regret all this, but it's too late to back out. She tries to sound demanding. "Him what?"

All she gets from Dusty is a glistening eye and a nod

toward the other one. She waits, but there is only silence and the creep of the shadows. She knows she will not get an answer until she turns and faces Mr. Cool. At last she does.

"He's going," he says.

She hears the words but they make no sense. "*Going?* Where?"

The kid finally looks away, which is a relief. He does his shrug thing. "Don't know."

The Dusty one wails: "He's going away! There's only gonna be two of us! Two Amigos!" He's not even pretending not to cry.

Ana Mae doesn't know what else to say, to think. She knows less now than she did before. *Going? How does a kid go? Why? To where?* She tries to think of another question but cannot. She foot-pushes her bike backward. She climbs into the saddle and slowly pedals away, toward nowhere in particular. *Going.* It doesn't make sense. She's never known a world without the Jack boy. Without all of them. Sure, she hates them. So does Jubilee. How many times have she and Jubilee wished they would all be trampled by the herd of wild bikes? But heck, the world is the world and boys are part of it, like flies. Without them, what would there be to swat?

In the distance she sees Jubilee tracing circles around Jack. It occurs to her that she may be looking at this whole thing the wrong way. Maybe she and Jubilee are getting their wish. If the shrugger and the crybaby are right, the population of the world is about to lose one boy. One boy down, one boy gone. That can't be bad.

Can it?

JUBILEE

*R*EMEMBER WHEN *we busted up our trikes?*

The words poke and sniff around the hatches of her brain, looking for a way in. They make no sense. Why would he say that to her? Why would he say anything to her except call her a name? They've never uttered a civil sentence to each other in their whole lives. What's he up to? Why is he acting so . . . so . . . un-Jack? Unboy?

Or is he?

Maybe she's underestimated boys. Or at least this one. Maybe there's actually a tiny speck of brain goop between the ears of this one. Maybe the whole thing is a trick. Maybe she's been looking at this whole thing the wrong way. When she awoke this morning and unspooned herself from Albert, there was the bike, the famous Scramjet, standing over her. Many times she had told the Jack kid she would ride his precious steed, just to rile him up. But she never really believed it. Now disbelief was mocking her: *Yo, Ace—who says you can't? It's easy. Mount up!* So she did, and all questions blew away with the wind in her hair.

Stolen? That's what they all thought: she stole it. But she didn't steal it. It came to her.

Or did it?

Maybe the Jack kid is just *acting* like he doesn't want his bike anymore. Maybe this whole thing from start to finish has been no accident. Maybe she's being set up. Maybe he snuck the bike over to her in the night where she was sleeping with Albert. Left it there for her to see when she awoke. Maybe he's smart enough to know she couldn't resist taking it. Keeping it. Yeah, maybe it's all just a big act. He's letting her *think* it's hers, letting her get attached to it, pretending he doesn't care. And then—*bam!*—he and his stupid Amigos will sneak in tonight when she's sleeping and snatch it right back. And wake up all of Hokey Pokey as they howl with laughter at their big joke.

She smiles to herself. *Good luck trying to get it back, A-meee-gos.*

He's at a distance now, but not too far. His jeans are crumpled around his sneaker tops. She calls: "Forget the trick, wormbrain! It's not gonna work!"

Strange, him not fighting back. In the old days he would turn and fire a word back at her, maybe even come stomping closer, the better to splash the word in her face. And the war would be on:

"Snotball!"

"Pimple!"

"Underwear breath!"

"Moron!"

Once, in a duel that became famous across the land, it went on all day long . . .

"Turdface!"

"Smello!"

"Baby!"

"Infant!"

. . . until night came and they both fell asleep, right there, half a spit from each other, firing away till the last drooping eyelid.

But no such thing now. He keeps on walking, giving no sign that he's heard her, leaving her no choice but to retreat to the last thing he said: *Remember when we busted up our trikes?* Yeah, she remembers. She remembers the satisfying crunch of trike on trike. She thought at first he was going to run off bawling. She's glad he didn't. That would have ruined everything. But he hung in there, climbed back in the saddle, came charging at her. By the time they were done, the trikes were wrecks and so were they, both of them wild-eyed and drooling, and she knew she had an enemy for life. Oh yeah, those were the days!

LOPEZ

FASTER.

Jack is going faster, a leaf on a current. Everything is faster, sharper. He can see the shadow of himself growing taller with every step. At this speed, he discovers, shadows can be heard: a faint scratching against the ground, as if an insect is crossing its legs. There's a breathy whisper in the air, but there is no wind here—it's the sun moving through the sky. Thunder booms beyond the Mountains.

The current brings him to the seesaw—and Lopez. She's crying.

"Don't cry," he says. He pulls down the high end,

sends her up, sits, anchors himself to keep her there. She loves up.

She's still crying.

"Don't go," she says. Her little cheeks are bright with tears.

"I'm not going anywhere," he says. "Where did you get that idea? Where would I go?"

The sound of his own question brings a new knowledge, smacks him in the face like a bad-hop grounder: *he's lying.* He knows it and she knows it. This is where all the strangeness has been leading. . . .

Sayonara, kid.

He remembers The Story:

One day when he woke up things were different.

The Kid was not himself.

I am going away.

The bike.

The tattoo.

The current.

The train whistle.

Tomorrow I will be gone.

The Kid says it in The Story. *Tomorrow.* Yesterday—all the yesterdays of his life—he did not know what it meant. Now he does. *Tomorrow.* A day that has not happened yet. Tomorrow morning—he knows this now, he saw it in Lopez's sad little face—tomorrow morning he will not wake up in Hokey Pokey. They seesaw without words. The only sound is the creak of the fulcrum. He doesn't stop till he sees that her tears have dried. Her eyes never leave him. She is memorizing his face.

One final bump to the ground and he dismounts. Down she comes. He grabs her and hoists her to his shoulders and gallops off. He can't see her face but he knows she is finally smiling, laughing, yippee-ki-yohing. She smacks his shoulder. "Giddyup, horsey!" He gallops her around Hippodrome, the kids on the painted wooden hippos crying out—"Me too! Me too!"—for a ride on Jack, and around Tantrums and its dome pipe puffing Category Two gas: violet. Now over to Cartoons and every little kid's dream: a hop onto the stage inches from the screen. Above them Bugs Bunny is chomping a carrot and drawling, "Ehh . . . what's up, Doc?" He holds Lopez so she can measure herself against Bugs's colossal foot—she's no bigger than his toe!

"Let's hokey pokey!" he says.

She laughs. "Jack, you can't make a circle with two."

"Is that so?" he says, and they do it—they make a circle of two:

Put your right foot in,
Put your right foot out . . .

And then he calls funny ones:

Put your right ear in . . .
Put your right armpit in . . .

When he calls the last one . . .

Put your right rump in . . .

. . . she's rolling on the ground, she's laughing so hard.
When he returns her to the seesaw, he does it quickly. She is flushed and giddy. It's been the experience of her life. He dumps her gently onto her seat. The word *goodbye* surges up his throat—he swallows it. He wants to hug her and never let go. But he knows he must leave her this way: deliriously, faintfully happy. As she makes Newbie-like gurble sounds, he touches his lips to the top of her head. He finds a rock, sets it on the other end in place of himself. She goes up, where she loves to be. She surveys Hokey Pokey. She smiles. He walks away. Runs away.

ALBERT, DESTROYER

WHERE AM I GOING?

Jack treads the dusty flats in a shower of calls—
"Hey, Jack! . . . Hey, Jack!"—but all he hears is *Where
am I going?*

The Hokey Pokey Man knows. Jack believes it. But
where is he? Where does the Hokey Pokey Man go after
the last kid is served? Jack wants to look. Wants to forget everything else and go searching and not stop until
he finds the Hokey Pokey Man, finds him so he can ask
Where am I going? But there is no time. It is time and
there is no time, and he must move. . . .

He lifts his shirt. Nothing. His stomach is as unmarked as a diapered Newbie's.

A breeze carries to him Hippodrome's tootle: *Hurry! . . . Hurry! . . .*

A commotion near Tantrums. Little kids are running and triking to a shallow gully, stopping at the rim, staring. Screams come from the gully. Jack quickens his pace. Kids stand aside to let him through. A little boy lies in the dust. He's curled into a ball. He's pulled his shirt up over his head. His screams are so forceful they blow a bulge in the make-do hood. Jack scans—no blood, no snakes. The gully is only a couple of feet deep, too shallow for the boy to have hurt himself falling into it. Jack feels a tug. He turns. A wide-eyed little girl is looking up at him, terrified. She sobs: "He got exploded!"

Jack laughs from relief. He jumps into the gully, touches the boy's bare shoulder. The boy cries, "No! No!" He peels the boy's fingers from the shirt, pulls it back down over his torso, gets a look at his face. Through its contortions of anguish he recognizes the face of the girl's brother. Albert. His cheeks are wet with tears, his nose snotty, his eyes clamped shut, and still he's screaming.

Jack shakes him. "Albert—stop! It's OK. It's me. Jack."

One eye opens. Then the other. Recognition. The screaming stops. Jack is figuring it's over when suddenly the kid starts in again, pulling his shirt over his head, wailing, "I'm exploded!"

The kid has curled himself into such a perfect ball that Jack is tempted to roll him up the gullyside. He manages to lug him up, but as he goes to dump the kid-ball onto the ground, two arms and legs spring out and now he's got an octopus clamping him in a death grip. "I'm exploded!"

Little kids circle closer, many of them sobbing too. Jack reminds himself to be gentle. The kid's terror is real. Jack lowers himself to the ground, gently pries the clutching limbs away, sits the kid on his lap, turns the kid's face to his. "Albert . . . Albert. Open your eyes. Look at me."

A little-girl voice wails, "Look at him, Albert!"

Like a pair of reluctant clams, the eyes open.

Jack takes it slow, soft: "You are *not* exploded. You're Albert. Same as always." He takes the kid's hand, dangles it in front of his face. "What's this?"

The kid snivels: "Hand."

"Whose hand?"

"My hand."

Jack pets the hand. "Exactly. See? You still have your hands, your feet. Your two ears." He waggles the kid's ears to prove it. Little kids laugh, grab their own ears. Albert laughs—and suddenly the clamshells shut and he's screaming again: "I'm exploded!"

Jack hauls himself and the kid up. "OK, that does it." He stomps off. This is something he probably should have done a long time ago. The mob parts. He addresses them all: "Where is he?"

Half of them pipe: "Over there!"

He follows the pointing fingers to the other side of Tantrums. There he is, the rogue runt who calls himself Destroyer, bullying some Snotsipper off his trike. When Albert spots him, he cries out and buries his face in Jack's neck. Jack walks up to the runt, who hasn't seen him yet. The Snotsipper is sobbing. Holding Albert with one hand, Jack reaches down with the other, grabs the back of the runt's shirt and plucks him off the trike. The runt shrieks in outrage, twists around, sees who's holding him and goes limp as a kitten in its mother's mouth. "Go," Jack tells the Snotsipper, who mounts his trike and churns away.

Jack sneers, "Destroyer, huh?" and dumps the runt on his butt. "Stay," he commands. He forces Albert to look down. "Doesn't seem so scary now, does he?"

Albert looks away.

Jack turns Albert's face toward the runt. Albert's eyes clamp shut.

"Open your eyes, Albert. Look at him. He's just a little kid like you. He's nothing to be afraid of."

Albert wails, "I can't!"

"You can."

"He'll explode me!"

Jack holds Albert at arm's length, shakes him. "He can't explode you if you don't let him. Watch this." He lowers Albert to the ground. He addresses the runt. "What's your real name?"

"Harold," the runt replies in a quivering peep.

"Harold," says Jack, "say hi to my friend Albert. Say *Hi, Albert*." Albert is cowering behind Jack's leg. "*Say* it."

"Hi, Albert."

"See, Albert," says Jack. "He talks, just like you. His nose is running, just like yours. He's just a kid, not a monster. Stand up, Harold." Harold stands. "Where's that thing you explode people with?" Harold pulls the yellow clicker from his pocket. Jack moves away from

Albert. "OK—explode me." The runt wags his head. "Don't tell me no. Explode me—*now!*"

The kid holds out the clicker. His arm is twitching. "Do it."

Albert wails, "Don't let him, Jack!"

A crowd is gathering. Several call out: "No, Jack!"

Jack levels a finger. "Do it." Sneers: "*Destroyer.*"

The kid squeezes the clicker.

"*Three* times. I know that's how you do it."

Click

Click

Click

Yelps from the crowd. Albert flinches, steps back, holds his ears, shuts his eyes. When he dares take a peek, amazement floods his face—Jack is still there!

"See?" says Jack. He holds out his arms for the world to see. He shakes his legs. He spins around. He does a tap dance. "Ta-da! I'm still here. Not exploded." He advances on Harold. "Gimme that." He snatches the clicker. He clicks it furiously into his own face: *Click Click Click Click Click Click Click Click* "See? Are my teeth falling out?" He shows his teeth, clacks them.

Nervous giggles from the gallery, from Albert. "No."

Without warning Jack whirls and fires a fast three

at Albert: *Click Click Click* The gallery gasps. Albert freezes, wide-eyed, stony as The Kid.

"How do you feel, Albert? Is your head still on? You still alive?"

Albert feels his head, checks himself all over. Grateful wonderment dawns. "I think so."

Jack triple-clicks Harold. Nothing happens.

Jack takes Albert by the hand, plants him in front of Harold. "Touch him, Albert. Reach out your hand and touch him."

Albert freezes.

"Touch him."

Albert reaches out, touches Harold's shoulder with a fingertip. Jack grabs Albert's hand, musses Harold's hair with it. In spite of himself, Albert giggles.

"See?" says Jack. "He's no monster. He's just another runt like you." He waves to the crowd. "Like you!"

The crowd applauds, whistles, cheers.

Jack drops the clicker to the ground. "Stomp it," he says.

"Now?" says Albert.

"Now. Stomp it."

Someone calls, "I'll stomp it!"

Albert stomps it. Five, six stomps. Mashes it into the dust.

"Kick it away."

He kicks the pieces away.

More cheers from the crowd.

"OK," says Jack. "Now come here, both of you." He pulls the two boys till they're face to face. "Albert, do you know why Harold here didn't get destroyed when I exploded him?"

Albert shakes his head. One hand is gripping Jack's pant leg.

"He didn't get destroyed because he doesn't believe it. See—he doesn't even believe himself. But"—he pokes Albert—"you did. If you believe it, it happens. If you don't, it doesn't. When you believe him, you put your own power in his hands. Got it, Albert?"

Albert nods.

"Got *what*?" Jubilee has tromped onto the scene.

"Jubee!" Albert runs, hugs her. "I'm not destroyed! Jack saved me!"

Jubilee picks up her brother, inspects him, puts him down. "That so?" Scowls at Jack. "If my brother needs to be saved, *I'll* save him. *You* mind your own business." She marches off, brother in one hand, bike in the other. Calls back: "And don't say his name!"

JACK

Kiki.

Lopez.

Albert.

He is swept along. Tumbleweed. No time to think. Just move. Go. Go. *To where?*

Hippodrome tootles.

A scuffed white soccer ball comes rolling. He does what he's done a thousand times, boots it, a long line drive. Twenty Snotsippers race after it, shrieking, laughing.

The world was once so simple. Gorilla Hill was

Gorilla Hill. The Wall was The Wall. Stuff was Stuff. Tantrums. Snuggle Stop. Jailhouse. Hippodrome. Cartoons. Sure, there were questions, but even they were a familiar part of the landscape, comforting if only because answers were always out of reach. How does The Story end? Do monsters exist? Where is The Kid pointing? What about the Hut?

Questions. Answers. Don't dump your marbles over a spit gob in the dust. What else was there to know?

Now. Then. New. Old.

He knows everything. He knows nothing. His shadow. His self. Shadowjack. Jackshadow. Leads. Follows. Spills. Bleeds. Shadowbleeds across the flats. Shadow stay. Jack go.

Where?

it's . . . time

Pinecones bounce off him. War rages. Trikes are tanks, pinecones grenades. M16s: *pow! pow! pow!* Machine guns nesting: *ack-ack-ack-ack-ack-ack-ack!* Paper Spitfire air cover. Bodies shot, reeling, falling, dead, rising, shooting, shot, reeling . . . death becomes life becomes death becomes . . . pinecones bounce. . . .

"Gotcha, Jack!"

"Yer blowed up, Jack!"

"Yer dead!"

"C'mon, Jack! Yer dead! Do it!"

He does it. One final time. His famous dead. Give them a going-away present. He reels, falls, sprawls on his back. Dead.

The sun purrs beyond his eyelids. He hears them running, shrieking, forgetting they're enemies.

"Look! It's Jack!"

"He's dead!"

"Go, Jack!"

He feels them gather round, feels their marveling stares, hears their breathings.

"He's dead all right."

"He's pretending."

"He is *not*! He's dead! Look—"

He feels a toetap to his foot. Someone barks: "Jack—wake up!"

"He ain't waking up. He's dead. Can'tcha see?"

"Look—he's not even breathing."

"Yes he is! I just saw his chest move!"

"No you didn't. Jack's the best deader there ever was."

Speculation and controversy swirl in the sunpurr. He has to force himself not to smile. Soon he senses nothing but awestruck reverence.

"Wow."

"How long can he do it?"

"Long as he wants."

"All day, if he wants."

"Man, that's *dead*."

"*Better* than dead."

And, as always happens, sooner or later somebody gets a little edgy, a little scared. "C'mon, Jack. You can wake up now. C'mon. Let's play."

He feels a finger poke to his upper arm, a toe poke to his thigh.

"C'mon, Jack. That's enough now."

Someone dares come close enough to gingerly lift his hand. It flops back to the dust. Someone moves his whole arm. It flops onto his stomach. Lifeless.

Till now it's been child's play. This is where he separates himself from even the great ones. They nudge him, flop his limbs this way and that, get down on their stomachs and inspect his chest for telltale motion.

"Tickle him!"

Someone always says it.

They do. First, tentative fingers brushing his ribs. And now, like always, they're on him like vultures on a carcass, tickling every patch of him. They would be astounded to know how easy this is for him to withstand. He was born without a tickle bone. It may be his greatest gift.

"Jack!"

As the ticklers back off, he recognizes the cry of Albert, the little brother.

"Jack! Wake up!" He feels himself shaken. He hopes the kid isn't too close, or he might catch one from that runny nose. "Wake up!"

Now—surprise—the girl's voice: "You heard him. Get up."

This is different. A new challenge. He sips in the last of his life signs till they are no more than a water-drop deep inside the dustflats of Jack.

"Wake him, Jubilee. I'm scared!" Albert.

A rude kick to his shoe. Another. "Now, meatball! Get up!"

Hiding in his waterdrop.

Silence now. What's happening? He feels something lightly on his chest. Little kids calling: "Kiss him! Kiss him!" He smells her, hears her breathing. She's close. *Very* close. And now she's gone, punching him in the shoulder. "Hah! I know you're in there. I could hear your heart beating. Game's over, nipplenose."

Hiding . . .

Now something heavy. She's sitting on him! Straddling his chest, squeezing his sipdrop of breath. She's tickling under his arms, his ribs. Now he feels her hair in his face, her ponytail faintly brushing like mosquitoes. He pictures the yellow ribbon. The crowd is going wild. "Go, Jubilee! Go, girl!" And now nothing but the weight on his chest. She's doing something. Desperately he wants to open his eyes, wants to see. "Kissee! Kissee!" His waterdrop freezes: *No!* But it's not a kiss he feels on his cheek (not that he knows what a girlkiss would feel like). It's a slap. And not just a light tap. A full roundhouse smack that rattles his skull and jolts his eyes open to the full face of the girl looming in place of the sky above him. Looming and smugly grinning: "Got-*cha*!"

He hears Albert cheer: "He's alive!"

The girl starts to climb off, pauses to smack him again. "Don't do it anymore, barfbrain. Not when my brother is around."

Jack jumps up, sends her tumbling. "Don't tell me what to do. And what do you care anyway?"

The girl picks herself up from the ground, seething. "I don't. But he does. He likes you. He's too young to know better. You ever make him cry again, you'll regret it."

"Oh yeah? What're you gonna do? Beat me up?"

She jaws up to him. "You think I can't? Huh? 'Cause I'm a girl? Huh?" She pokes him in the chest, sends him backward.

He counterpokes, countersneers. "I don't beat up girls. It's too easy."

She laughs. In the background the sidekick Ana Mae brays: "Waste him, Ace!"

She pokes him again. She scuffs dust onto his sneaks. She jabs him in the stomach. "Let's go, mucho macho. A-*meeee*-go. Let's see how *eeeeas*y it is." She bops him on the nose.

It's the craziest thing, but instead of whacking her one, he feels like laughing. He feels like standing here for a while and letting her bop away. Suddenly he reaches out, his arm acting on its own. He sees the jolt in her eyes, fright even. He wants to say *Don't worry,* but it's all happening so fast. His hand is reaching behind her head and snatching the yellow ribbon and he's running off, the girl screaming after him, the mob going bonkers.

AMIGOS

T**HEY'RE COMING OUT OF THE SUN**, so he hears them before he sees them.

"Yo! Jack!"

He sees now that the heatshimmering clot between them is a third bike. He stops, waits.

Dusty's eyes are bright with excitement. "Saddle up, Jack!" He wheels up an ancient nag.

"Where'd you get this?"

"It was by itself. Nobody was watching. We'll take it back. C'mon, hop on." The bike tilts as Dusty releases it. Jack grabs it.

"What's this about?"

"One last roundup. We just thought it would be fun."

"What do you mean *one last?*"

"Since you're going away."

Jack feels a chill. Somehow it's OK for him to know—but *them?* "Who says I'm going away?"

Dusty appears startled. He glances at LaJo, back to Jack. "Ain'tcha?"

Jack looks at LaJo. LaJo shrugs. Jack doesn't know what to say, doesn't even know what he thinks. He echoes LaJo's shrug. "Whatever." He saddles up. "No rope," he says.

"LaJo, give him yours," says Dusty. LaJo unties his own from the crossbar, tosses it. Jack is touched. His Amigos. They never forget him. They're the best pals a kid could have. They ride off to Great Plains.

They find the herd milling in the shadow of the Plains' only tree, a black jagged monstrosity clawing at the sky like upchucked evil.

"We'll circle around this way," says Dusty. "You go that way. Pick one out and go after him."

Jack is impressed with Dusty, who's suddenly become a take-charge guy. He circles around the herd at a distance so as not to spook them. Though he didn't have to capture Scramjet, he and the Amigos have spent many happy hours chasing down mustangs, roping them, then letting them go free and wild for another day. He's glad his pals thought of this. Just like old times.

Usually they would go after a slow-wheeling nag or unsavvy youngster, easier to catch them. But this time—will it really be the last roundup?—he figures he'll do it right, show the herd the respect it deserves. And right away he spots the prize. A proud stallion—not another Scramjet, of course, but a red-and-gray beauty, that mix of arrogance and can-do that defines the true thoroughbred, tall, wary, protecting its harem of three or four mares. Dusty and LaJo are saddlesitting, watching, letting him have the fun. He approaches at an angle, slowly coasting, not even looking at the stallion, trying to send the message: *Hey, I'm just another easy loper on the open range*. But of course that doesn't work for long. The beauty's got his head up now; he's turning, pawing at the turf. A nicker, a nip at a mare's flank, a flash of chrome—and they're off, the whole herd reeling sideways as if smacked by a wind. The chase is on!

The dust is choking him. He's an expert nostril-tapping snot-shooter, so he has no booger-need for a hankie. The one in his back pocket is for times like this. He pulls it out. He triangulates it, ties it around his face like a bandito mask and breathes again. His pulse is singing with the chorus of a hundred spinning wheels, the seat untouched beneath his flying butt. "Heeeeee-yah!" he rejoices, and beyond the dust hears his cry rebound: *Heeeeee-yah!* The Amigos ride again!

He shouts: "The red and gray!"

Hears Dusty's callback: "I see 'im!"

Kids. Bikes. Dust. The eternal whirlwind scores the Plains.

Jack longs for Scramjet. What a cinch this would be then. At least this rattletrap loaner isn't falling to pieces beneath him.

The red and gray, as if knowing he's the prize, holds to the middle of the pack. Jack churns on, pulls up beside a straggler, an old mare clattering and spitting rubber and in its panic losing its saddle, which now looks like a cockeyed beret. Jack tilts to the right, slaps his own flank—"Hee-yah!"—forces the mare to veer another way.

One by one he picks up others, peels them off the beeline. To his left Dusty and LaJo are doing likewise, all three slapping thighs, yelling "Hee-yah!" Within minutes the target is running solo, boring ahead as if to drill a hole in the Mountains. His Amigos pull back. Jack knows Dusty is readying his rope, but it's just for backup—this is Jack's party. Guiding the wheels with no more than a fingertip, he lets out a few coils of rope, shakes and widens the loop, pulls up on the left flank of the galloping stallion. He drags the loop behind, feels the windwhipped tremble in the rope, draws a bead on the flashing handlebars, is about to heave when . . . when . . . he's . . . *roped?* A looped rope falls over his own shoulders, tightens, pins his arms to his sides. Suddenly he's riding with no hands, something he's done countless times but always by choice. That stupid moron Dusty has gone and overexcited himself and tried to lasso the bronc and wound up roping Jack instead. As the red and gray pulls away, Jack tries to work his arms free but finds he cannot, the rope is holding tight. "You nitwit!" He screams so forcefully his hankie falls from his nose. "Let me go! He's getting away!"

He feels a stronger tug, pulling him to a stop. Dusty and LaJo are beside now, each taking a handlebar so he won't fall. "You idiots! I was just—" He's spouting words that even he doesn't understand, because instead of loosening the rope and letting him get on with the chase, they're riding circles around him, coiling the rope from shoulders to belt until he's feeling like some kind of open-range mummy. "What the—" OK, now he gets it. It wasn't a mistake at all, it's a joke. And if he's honest, a pretty good one. "OK, you morons, congratulations on your big funny. Ha-ha. I'm laughing. OK? Now let me go."

He's talking to them, he's looking at them, he's looking into their eyes, but they're not looking at him. They're looking at the rope, at the bike, at the sky, anywhere but into his face. "Hey! Hel-*lo*?" he yells, but they seem not to hear. He's never seen their faces like this.

They tie the rope end to the bike, pull everything so tight the bike feels like an extra leg. Now they tilt the whole thing over and lower him slowly—he notices the care they take—to the ground. He's looking up at them now. He's resting on his left ear. He sees the world sideways. He's speechless. He's run out not only of words but of thoughts. He squints in the blinding sun. He's lost his cap. LaJo fetches it, replaces it carefully on his head, pulls the brim down good and low, shading his eyes.

They stand above him. He has this weird feeling that he's in a picture looking out at them. He feels a question coming, but it's Dusty who speaks: "Sorry, Amigo." The strange look is gone from Dusty's face now. He seems a little scared, a little sad.

"I told you we shouldna done it," says LaJo.

"Done what?" says Jack, which is not precisely the word he wants. "*Why?*"

"It's just for now," says Dusty finally, looking nowhere but deep into his eyes. "We'll stay here with you the whole time, Amigo. Don't worry. We'll sleep with you the whole night. Some kinda trick's going on. We'll figure it out. Soon as you're back to yourself— *bam*—we let you go."

JACK

Is keeping his eyes shut. He doesn't even want to see these nincompoops. He hears LaJo say, "Take his hankie off."

And Dusty say, "What for?"

"Just do it."

He feels Dusty's hands untying the hankie from behind his neck. Now he's too curious; he has to peek. Sideways, he sees LaJo's hands fold the hankie. He feels one hand gently lift his head while the other does something. When he lays his head back down, the folded hankie is between himself and the ground. It feels better. A little. The shadow of his face spills into the dust.

He recloses his eyes, hears Dusty: "Not good enough." Hears Dusty mount his bike and ride off. He opens his eyes. LaJo is sitting five feet away, elbows propped on knees, staring at him.

"Let me go," he says.

LaJo puts on his downmouth, shakes his head.

"Why not?"

Shrug.

"You already said you shouldna done it. So *undo* it. Untie me."

"No can do."

"LJ. Amigo."

LaJo winces.

"Amigo. Amigo. Amigo."

LaJo gets up, walks off.

"Wait! Don't go. You can't leave me."

LaJo stops, speaks to the Mountains. "I ain't leaving you. Don't worry."

He knows this is true. Whatever crazy thing is going on, they will never leave him here alone. And thinks: *Bad luck, to be stuck with LaJo. Dusty can be talked into anything.*

"LaJo."

"Huh?"

"What's this about? Why are you doing this?"

LaJo's shoulders go up, down.

"Don't shrug at me, man. Tell me."

LaJo turns, looks down at him. He can tell LaJo hates seeing him this way, hog-tied, helpless, his old best pal.

"*Tell* me."

"Ask Dusty."

"I'm asking *you*. You're ticking me off now, man. I got rights. You can't do this to me and not tell me why. Tell me or let me go—*now*."

LaJo shrugs. "Simple. We keep you here, you can't go nowhere."

They know but they don't know. They don't understand. Heck, neither do I.

"You think I'm going somewhere."

"Yeah."

"OK, so where do you geniuses think I'm going?"

Shrug. "Away."

Away. The answer he himself would have given. But *where*? "Away where?" he says, and sees how crazy this is becoming: he's so starved for answers he's trying to get them from LaJo.

Of course LaJo's answer is a shrug.

"So you're just gonna keep me here?" says Jack.

"For now."

"Now."

"Yeah."

"And what comes after now?"

LaJo looks at him, looks away. He's too bewildered to even shrug.

Jack ponders. A question comes. He's afraid to ask it. But does: "LJ . . . what if I *do* go . . . away? What're you afraid of? What do you think's gonna happen then?"

He's never seen LaJo flustered like this before. LaJo looks like he's just kicked over a rock and out comes crawling this word he's never seen before: "Then? . . . *Then? . . .*"

Jack feels pity, almost smiles, thinks: *It's in The Story, LJ. It's called tomorrow.*

Back to square one. "LaJo. Let me go."

"No."

"Why?"

"Can't."

"Why?"

"Dusty."

"Dusty?"

"Dusty said."

"Since when do you do what Dusty says?"

"Since now."

This is the true—and scary—measure of LaJo's desperation: he's taking orders from Dusty.

"So when are you gonna let me go? When *Boss Dusty* says?"

LaJo's stare burns through his shirt to his bare stomach. "When you're back to yourself."

The Kid was not himself.

Jack knows that, despite his Amigos' fears and gallant efforts, the current cannot be stopped. All day long Jack—not just his tattoo but Jack's whole self, bit by bit—has been disappearing into The Story. He can't imagine how things will happen from this moment on, but happen they will. The Story cannot be untold.

And yet . . . his fingernails rake the motherdust of Hokey Pokey . . . he is still *here*, it is still what it has always been: *today.*

"So I'm going away, huh?"

LaJo shrugs. "Not if we can help it."

How he loves these guys.

He doesn't want to do it, but he has to. He's become The Story. "LaJo. Look at me."

LaJo sends him one glance and turns his back. But

not before Jack caught the terror in LaJo's eyes. Confused as he is, he senses what Jack is going to say. He thinks words cannot penetrate a turned back. But they can, and Jack cannot stop them. He's not quoting now, he's saying: "*I am going away.*"

He waits for a reaction, but the shoulders are unmoved. He speaks now with great gentleness. "So . . . LaJo . . . c'mon. Give it up. Let me go. It's time."

Now he sees LaJo's shoulders stiffen. And now LaJo is charging, screaming: "Shut up! Shut up! You don't know what you're talking about!" LaJo stomps around behind him and kicks him in the butt. "You're gonna be OK! We're all gonna be OK! We're gonna wake up and do our Tarzan yells and ride our bikes and chase the herd and mess around and everything's gonna be the way it's s'pose to be! So shut up or I swear I'm gonna gag ya!"

If he wasn't so shell-shocked, Jack might break out laughing. And he's thinking about laughing anyway when he sees Dusty heading this way in the distant heatshimmer. Except now he sees it's not just Dusty biking this way. Another black dot appears on the horizon. Someone is following Dusty.

AMIGOS, GIRL

Iᴛ's ᴛʜᴇ ɢɪʀʟ.

Dumb Dusty of course doesn't even know he's being followed. He pulls up with a catcher's mitt in one hand, beaming. "Your pillow, Amigo!" He removes the hankie and slips the mitt beneath Jack's left ear. "Presto! You'll sleep like a baby."

He's right, it feels great, but Jack is not about to admit it. "Where'd you get it?" he says.

"I borrowed it." All proud of himself. "Don't worry. I'll give it back."

It strikes Jack that they keep saying *Don't worry*. It strikes him that for the second time today Dusty has become a thief for him. It strikes him that, despite his ridiculous predicament, he might say thank you. But he doesn't. He says, "Maybe you should borrow something from *her*."

Dusty, slow as always, frowns in confusion. And practically electrifies when he hears the voice behind him: "What are you doing to him?"

LaJo chuckles.

"They're holding me hostage," says Jack.

The girl smirks. "Do tell." She turns to LaJo. "Why?"

LaJo nods at Dusty. "Ask him."

She doesn't bother to ask again. Obviously she doesn't care why. She's just delighted to see him this way. She parks the yellow bike, once his Scramjet. She kneels before him. She checks the ropes, mutters to herself, "No joke." The more she looks, the wider her grin gets. He hears tiny giggles. He has the impression this is the happiest moment of her life. She presses his nose with her fingertip, peeps: "Boop!"

And now she's going through his pockets. She pulls out the yellow ribbon. "Did you really think you could steal this from me?" She sneers out the next word: "A-*meee*-go?" She turns her back on him so he can watch her tie the ribbon to her hair, repony the tail.

He figures she's about to go, but she surprises him.

225

She plops her butt in the dust and stares at him, her delight endless. Finally she looks up at Dusty. "So—why?"

Unlike Jack and LaJo, Dusty sometimes actually speaks to girls in a normal voice, but this girl has him practically peeing his pants. Dusty looks to LaJo, but LaJo offers only a scowl. "It's hard to explain," he croaks. His chin is quivering.

The girl sneers, "You're not gonna cry on me, are ya?"

He lashes out: "Cry? Waddaya mean cry? I don't cry."

"So what're you afraid of? Why did you do this to your A-*meee*-go?"

Dusty squeaks, "I ain't afraida nothin. It's hard to explain, that's all."

For a while everybody just blinks at each other. There's no sound, not even the tootle of Hippodrome, which is too far away. Then, out of nowhere, LaJo speaks: "The Story."

The girl stares. "Huh?"

"The Story. You know The Story, don't you?"

The girl stands. "Yeah, I know The Story. So what's that got to do with the price of beans?"

LaJo glances at Jack. "It's happening to him."

It's paining Jack's neck to keep the girl's face in view, but he wants to see it now more than ever. Her face is a story. Now that he thinks of it, he's always noticed that about her. It's like she doesn't even have to speak. If you want to know what she's thinking or what she's about to say, just read her face. It's there.

And what he sees now is that she's thinking about The Story. She's hearing it again in her walnut shell. She's paging through it, episode by episode, and so is he. The time The Kid rode his tricycle down Gorilla Hill and hit a rock and went flying over the handlebars. The time The Kid threw a stone at a groundhog and knocked it out and held it in his lap and cried until the groundhog came to. The time the kids of Hokey Pokey tricked him out to Thousand Puddles and torture-tickled and mudded him into a statue so he wouldn't go away.

He thinks: *At least they didn't take me out to Thousand Puddles.*

She looks at him, grins, touches him with her sneaker toe. "At least they didn't turn you to dried mud." She smirks. "So what're you saying? The Kid's come back?"

"It's no joke!" Dusty cries.

LaJo faces the Plains, speaks as if to the tumbleweed: *"One day when he woke up . . ."*

The girl stares at LaJo, follows his gaze across the Plains, finds the rest of the words among the purple sage, whispers: ". . . *the tattoo was gone.*" She kneels before Jack. With great delicacy she takes the hem of his shirt between thumb and fingertip and slowly lifts it. What she sees makes her gasp. She releases the shirt. She falls back. The shadow of the brown bird races between them.

JUBILEE

Gₑₜₛ ᵤₚ, ᴅᴀᴢᴇᴅ. Walks. Walks. The open range yawns.
They cannot take their eyes from her.

They watch her walk in the sun, in the dust. The
figure of her becomes smaller with each step. They see
her stop. Stop and stand still: girl, tumbleweed, Great
Plains, Mountains. She does not move and she does
not move. What does she see? What does she hear?
They see something, on the ground in front of her, a
little something. A prairie dog. It has come up from its
hole in the dust. It seems to be standing on its hind
legs, facing her, not running. Perhaps it is unafraid

because she is so still. Or perhaps there is something about her. As they watch the two of them in the distance, they begin to believe that the girl and the prairie dog are not just facing each other in silence. They begin to believe that one or perhaps both of them are speaking.

AMIGOS

No one has spoken since the girl walked off, until now. Suddenly Dusty won't shut up. "What're we—crazy? Look! She left her bike here—*your* bike, Jackaroo—and we ain't even doin nothin about it. We're a disgrace." He kicks dust over the tires.

"So if it's Jack's," says LaJo, "why are you kicking dirt all over it?"

Dusty's hand goes to his mouth. "Oops." He rushes to the bike, brushes off dirt with his hand. "Well, she ain't getting it back. That dumb chick's messin with the wrong dudes." He wrenches off the pink handlegrips, flings them in the direction of the departed girl. "Mucho mistako, chico! Don't mess with the Amigos!"

"Put 'em back," says Jack, loving Dusty for fighting the unfightable.

Dusty turns, points. "No way, Jack." He rips tufts of white fuzz from the seat cover. "We're gonna paint him, Jack. Just like he was. Black and silver." He takes one smart step back. He salutes. "Scramjet rules!"

"It's hers now," says Jack. He's feeling weary, tired of talking about the same thing, tired of being in the same place. He needs to move.

Dusty turns on him. "Don't *say* that! The bike is yours and you ain't goin *nowhere*."

Jack lays his head on the mitt, closes his eyes. Soon he hears LaJo, the smirk in his voice: "You're grass now, Dustman. Here comes the lawn mower."

JACK

Eʏᴇs ᴛʜᴇ ɢɪʀʟ's ʀᴇᴛᴜʀɴ. He feels a fillip of fear for Dusty, for he knows how ornery this girl can be. But she merely glances at the desecrated bike and keeps coming, straight to him. She kneels. She tilts her head to align her eyes with his. She stares. She says, "You *really* going away?"

He nods against the mitt, smells the sweet leather, the scent of his life.

"Is *that* why the tattoo is gone?"

"I guess so."

"When did it happen?"

"Today. All day."

"When are you going?

"Tonight . . . I think."

"How do you know?"

"I don't. It's like"—he stares up into her eyes—"I'm on a bike I can't steer, can't stop."

"So . . . ," she says, "where *to?*"

He hangs full-weight from her eyes. "Beats me."

Somewhere in the space between them their eyes meet and something happens. He doesn't know what it is. He only knows it's never happened before and it's not a bad thing.

She doesn't speak. She reaches out. Someone yips, "Hey—" but that's all. She unties him from the bike. She tosses the rope over her shoulder. It lands at LaJo's feet. She stands. He stands. He rubs his wrists, flexes his legs, straightens his cap.

She turns and goes to the bike. She makes no attempt to retrieve the pink handlegrips. She walks the bike away. He rights his borrowed nag and follows. No one speaks.

POCKETS

THEIR FOOTFALLS are the only sounds upon the land.
Shadows spill from sage and tumbleweed.

"You can have your bike back," she says.

"It's yours now," he says.

"I didn't steal it."

"I know."

"Really."

"I know."

"I *thought* about it a million times."

He grins. "I know."

"I came close once."

"Yeah?"

"Yeah. I found it parked by the sliding board. I was going to take it, but I chickened out. But I *did* do something."

"What?"

"I spit on the seat. Probably the biggest slobber-bomb I ever dropped. It was so big some of it even spilled over. Remember?"

He nods, remembering. "Yeah. Shoulda known that was you."

She grins, looks at him. "What did you think? Were you mad?"

He grins. "Not at first."

"Why not?"

"I didn't see it." He looks at her. "Then I sat in it."

They howl.

"I hated you," she says.

"You hated all boys," he says.

"Yeah. But I hated you the most."

He feels chesty, as if a general has just pinned a medal on him. But also a little sad. "I hated you too."

They walk on, out of Great Plains, into Hippodrome's tootle range. War rages ahead of them. Tank trikes. Pinecone grenades. *Pow! Pow! Pow!* Golden guns spout red streamers of caps, burp the sweet burn of powpowder.

Jack wades in. Jubilee starts to follow, now stays, sensing this is his. A grenade bounces off Jack's head. He picks it up, tosses it over his shoulder. Everyone falls dead. Standing tall amid the carnage, Jack reaches into his pocket, says, "OK, who wants something?"

Bodies spring up, surround him.

"What, Jack, what?"

He pulls out his prize marble, his master mib. He won it as a Gappergum and has been winning with it ever since. He holds it up between two fingers, but even in the full light of the sun the murky blue-gray swirl obscures the center, a mystery he has been sorely tempted to solve by cracking the mib but could never bring himself to do. He is content to believe he holds in his hand, encapsulated, the very birth moment of the universe.

A dozen tongues wag, two dozen hands reach. "Me, Jack, me!"

He plunks the marble into the nearest hand. The kid flies off shrieking.

Next out of the pocket is his lucky stone. Pink quartz. He remembers the day he got it. He was exploring down by the creek and he spotted it in the water. He took one step to the right to pick it up, and just then a rotten branch from a tree fell where he had been standing. From then on he never went anywhere without that stone. And never saw another one like it. He hands it to a kid.

Next, his rock-hard wad of bubble gum. It's his standby lucky stone, just in case he ever lost the real one. He's glad he never had to put the gum stone to the test. Another kid runs off cheering.

One by one the priceless treasures of his pockets fall to the groping, ecstatic Snotsippers: raven's feather, mystery tooth, four-leaf clover, root beer root, cat hair ball, scrap of shed garter-snake skin, mummified salamander, petrified snake turd, two-headed raisin.

He stands alone, his pockets empty except for the walnut shell. That he'll keep.

Jubilee joins him. "What was that about?"

"Gave away my stuff."

"Why?"

He thinks about it. "I don't know."

"Don't you want to take your stuff wherever you're going?"

He looks at her, blinks, looks away, shrugs.

JACK, JUBILEE

"LET'S RIDE," she says.

"Good idea," he says.

She leans the bike toward him. "One last time?"

He snorts in mock contempt. "Me? On a yellow bike? Named Hazel?"

They laugh.

They ride.

They reach out and flick the DON'T sign as they pass, making it flutter.

They circle Tantrums, the dome pipe now puffing Category Three gas: aqua.

"This way," says Jack. He leads her beyond Tantrums, to the excavation site. Mitchell seems to have the massive fossil complete and upright now. He's chipping at the spokes.

Jubilee gasps. "Wow!" She dismounts. "What is it?"

"Not sure," says Jack. "I think it's the bones of some giant extinct bike, some species that doesn't exist anymore. Big, huh?"

Jubilee fifes a wonderwhistle. The dug-up bike stands above them, on a low hummock. She kickstands Hazel and approaches carefully. She stands beside the gray, stone-crusted colossus. She stiffens to attention. "Look!"

It's amazing. The top of her head falls well short of the top of the front fender. When she raises her hand, her fingers waggle far below the handlebar. She bounds back down the hill. "D'ja see?"

Jack nods. "Yeah. It's something, huh?"

They ride. A siren floods the land with three short guttural bursts: *Bawlk! Bawlk! Bawlk!* Silence. Then three more bursts.

"Badword jailbreak," says Jack.

Jubilee nods. "Did one ever catch you?"

Jack nods sheepishly. "Yeah. Couple times."

"Me too," says Jubilee.

They head for Hippodrome, where they dismount for a spin on the hippos. Normally only Sillynillies and smaller can ride a mouth, but Jack and Jubilee find a pair of yawning maws they can squeeze into. The little kids go wild at the sight of two Big Kids joining them.

They ride their bikes onto the stage at Cartoons, dismount, tap-dance, bow, exit to cheers and whistles.

They pull up to Snuggle Stop. "One last time," he says, and goes in. Comes out. "That was good."

They ride through Doll Farm . . . Trucks. He laughs. "That time you came after me with the fire truck and aimed the hose at me and nothing came out."

She laughs. "The time you stole my football and I chased you all the way to the creek and you threw it in the water and it floated away. You thought I was going to cry."

He grins at the memory. "But you didn't."

"Nope."

"You never cried."

"Neither did you."

"Boys aren't supposed to."

"Little boys are."

"Sometimes I did, when you weren't around."

"Sometimes I did too, when you weren't around."

He chuckles. "I used to think: *A girl that don't cry. She can't be real.*"

She looks at him. "So what do you think now?"

He looks. The ribbon ends peek from behind her cap. "Yeah, you're real."

She grins. "Race!"

They race across the flats. Dust boils. Jack's nag is no match for his old Scramjet. They slow to a biketrot, laughing.

"Follow me," he says. He leads her to The Kid. He kickstands the nag. "I need my old bike." She hands it over. He stands in the stirrups, balances, wobbles, stills himself, whispers, "Steady, boy, steady." He hauls one foot onto the saddle. Now both. Crouching. Arms out, teetering. Wobble . . . wobble. She reaches to steady the bike. "No!" he says. "I'll be OK. He knows it's me." Slowly, carefully, he straightens until he's standing tall in the saddle. He reaches up, almost to the outstretched arm, the pointing finger. He jumps, curls both hands around the arm. "OK—pull it away." She pulls the bike away. "Count," he says. She counts aloud as he does five chin-ups on the arm. He releases, drops to the dust, gasping: "Alwayswanted . . . todo . . . that."

They ride.

Around Socks . . . past Tattooer . . . in and out of the junky mounds of Stuff.

"I never hit you," she says, marvel in her voice.

"So?" he says. "What're you saying? You wish you did?"

"No. Just I'm surprised we never hit each other. Since we hated each other so much."

He shrugs. "No big deal. I'm not much of a hitter anyway. I was probably afraid you'd hit me back and make me cry."

They laugh. They ride.

He blocks her with his arm. "Stop!"

"What?" she says.

"This." He nods. Before them is Flowers. The little square plot of soil is gashed with footprints and tire tracks. Flowers lie like dead soldiers. One remains standing in a corner. Jack resumes riding, steers carefully around the plot. Hesitating, Jubilee follows. They ride a brief way when Jack stops again.

"What now?" she says.

Jack says nothing, seems at a loss for words. He stares at her, looks behind. He dismounts and walks back to the patch. He kneels before the last flower. He looks at it, closely. He's never done such a thing before. There are white petals surrounding a round, dusty yellow button. He counts the petals. Nine of them. He wonders if the flower has a name. Something in him wants to pick it, perhaps give it, but in the end he lets it be. He returns to his bike.

"What was that all about?" she says.

He has no answer. They ride away.

They hear shrieks in the distance. A herd of Gappergums is racing across the flats followed by a badword—barnacled, feelers flailing—followed by a flapping pelican—the warden—mouth pouch skimming the ground, ready to scoop. They halt to watch.

"The jailbreaker," says Jack.

"Ten-legger," says Jubilee.

They resume their ride.

"I almost called you that once," he says.

Jubilee is shocked. "Really? You hated me *that* much?"

Jack backtracks. "No, no, I would never really say it. It just popped into my head once."

They ride in silence for a while, giving the thing time to blow away. Eventually she chuckles.

"What?" he says.

"Just thinking."

"What?"

"Some stuff *I* could have said. Never did."

He nods, smiling. "Yeah. Me too."

"Once"—she chuckles—"once I was going to dare you to do something."

"What?" he says.

"I was going to dare you to bend over backwards with your hands flat on the ground."

"Why?"

She shrugs. "Just to show you that you couldn't and I could. You were always acting like you could do everything and girls can't."

"Really? That's how I acted?"

They're riding side by side. She looks at him. "Yeah." Suddenly she stops, dismounts. She stands, legs spread slightly, and cranks herself back slowly until her palms press firmly into the ground. Her thighs and belly make a table. Her cap falls off. The end of her ponytail kisses the dust. She straightens up with a grunt, retrieves her cap.

Jack claps, says, "You win."

"I know," she says brightly, and they ride off.

He begins laughing. He can't stop.

"What?"

"I'm just thinking . . . do you remember—you were pretty little—remember finding your doll one day with its head off?" He's grinning at her.

She turns to him slowly, memory emerging from the fog. *"You?"*

He nods. She punches his arm. They ride.

"I could've messed up your bike," she calls over the windwhistle, ponytail flying.

"I could have knocked that green hokey pokey out of your hand," he counters.

"I could have put mud in the fingers of your precious baseball glove."

"I could have kidnapped your little brother."

Ahead of them, crossing their path: two runners. A tiny red-haired one chasing a big brown one. Jack laughs. He's heard about this. "It's LaJo," he says. "Got stuck with a first-day Newbie."

LaJo is pulling away but the Newbie—"LaJo! LaJo!"—isn't giving up.

They laugh. They ride.

"I didn't know there was so much stuff we didn't do," she says.

"Me neither," he says.

"Too bad."

"Yeah."

"Too late now, huh?"

He doesn't answer.

"Another thing," she says.

"What?"

"I never tried a root beer hokey pokey."

"Really? Never?"

"Everything but."

"It's my favorite."

She skirts a tumbleweed. "I know."

They stop. Stay. The sun perches on a mountain, a raspberry hokey pokey melting across land and sky. A dandelion puff floats by.

They ride. They're heading for the red bluff.

They circle the blackberry bramble. "Hey," he says. "Let's do Gorilla Hill!"

As they have often done separately, they get a running start and pedal furiously up the hill but only make it halfway. No one has ever pedaled to the peak. They walk their bikes the rest of the way. They linger at the top, surveying the land. Behind them are the tracks, the creek, the jungle. Before them Hokey Pokey sprawls to the Mountains. They can see all the way to Thousand Puddles and Trucks. They can see the mustang herd moving across Great Plains, the big round button of Tantrums, Cartoons' giant screen. And everywhere: kids.

"It's all so little from up here," she says.

"Yeah," he says. He points. "Look—"

She looks, smiles. "Circle. And look—another."

They keep finding them:

"Three!"

"Four!"

"Five!"

Kids in circles dancing the hokey pokey all over the place. Laughter and words ride thistledown up the slope:

Put your left foot out . . .

"Best time to do it," she says.

"Sundown," he says. And catches his breath. It's the sound. He hesitates, asks her, "Hear it?"

She looks at him. She listens. "What?"

"Whistle. Train."

"But—" she starts to say, and stops. She leans into her handlebars, bows her head, closes her eyes. He's never seen anyone listen so hard. Nor, when she at last looks up, has he ever seen eyes so sad. She shakes her head.

The sun has rolled down the far side of the Mountains.

He crunches his pedal. "You first!" he says.

She doesn't argue. One push-off and she's zooming down the hill. He follows in her dust, both of them pitching wild, primal screams across the land. They coast onto the flats, turn back up the hill and do it again. And again. And again. They switch: he goes first, she goes first. There is no talking, only the screaming and the flushed faces and, as they coast the flats side by side, a silence of more words than they have spoken in all their lives.

Each time they cross the flats, the shadows are longer. Over the shoulder of the Mountains the sun heaves the last of its light. Hokey Pokey is golden.

Jack looks up. The moon is out. And the first star. He feels a chill. He looks at her. "I gotta go," he says.

"But—" she says.

"It's time."

They walk their bikes toward the bluff. Crickets *clickit.*

They stop at the blackberry bramble. Jack parks his bike. "Guess I'll just leave it here," he says. "Somebody will take it."

"I'll tell them Jack rode it," she says. "They'll fight over it."

They walk to the edge of the bluff. Below them, the

tracks emerge from the trees on one end and vanish into the trees on the other end.

"Is there really a train?" she asks him.

He nods. "Yeah."

They stand silently at the rim. "I can't come, can I?" she says.

"Not now," he says.

"I don't understand," she says.

"Neither do I," he says.

The brown bird flies in the twilight.

He sighs. "Well—"

"Well—" she says. Her eyes are brimming.

He starts to go.

She calls, "Jack—wait!"

She comes to him. She unwraps the yellow ribbon from her hair. She holds it out. He takes it, stares at it, puts it in his pocket. And he is gone, slipsliding down the steep bluffside, two hops over the tracks and into the trees.

She calls, "Albert will miss you!" She hopes for a last glimpse, a flash of his cap, but through her tears she can see nothing but shadows and green.

JACK

Eᴍᴇʀɢᴇs ꜰʀᴏᴍ ᴛʜᴇ ᴛʀᴇᴇs onto the creek's stony apron. On the island before him stands the ramshackle Forbidden Hut. He sloshes through the water, ignoring stepping-stones. He is not thinking, just doing. Something has awakened in his blood, voicelessly guiding him. He doesn't even pause at the door. The shiny brass knob turns easily in his hand. The door creaks open, cobwebs shred. In the dying daylight he makes out a dirt floor, nail-pocked, mouldering walls. The only object seems to be a rectangular metal cabinet as tall as himself. It is framed in tiny red lights that twinkle. It is otherwise gray and faceless except for two small open-ings: one round, the other a slit. Except for the twin-kling cabinet, the place is dreary and unremarkable, not at all what he has always imagined. It has the faintly rotting smell of muck.

He knows exactly what this place is. It is the station.

And now he begins to hear a new sound. At first he assumed it was the rush of creekwater. But no—it is something else. It is like many things. It is like wind in the trees. It is like the panting of a thousand puppies. It is like the hum of things unknown. But it is none of these. It is names. Names and names and names, swarm-ing through the gloom, bouncing off the walls, winged whisperings by the millions, an eternity of names:

LanaPercyAmyHildegardeJillianPeterHerman AngelJaniceReynaldoLucyRobertChoiWandaJohn EstherToyaBernardIvanPierreMargueriteFantasia BorisMaudeSolomonJoshuaOdetteEthelRyanBrod VirginiaJamesNatalieMiaChloeZackRussellSummer TaylorKevinXavierTimothyThomasMarySashaBen GwenHaroldOrmorodBillLeslieHeatherGiselleWill AnthonyIldikoMarinaLarryClaireLeahDonaldWilson SvenSarahMitchellNoreenYvonneBrookeDavid

YasmirEileenGeorgeJenniferSeanJoelEdwinIsabel
BarbaraJeffreySukiSamMollyHelenRogerCourtney
AllieKatherineWalterIngridKeithPattyLuluSalome
PedroOkalaniKofiDannyKonstantinBobAmanda
NinaTaoMichelleCosmoKatieEmilyAhmedJanet
CalliopeKennyLenaBruceAshtonAshleyEmma
MarkAvaOrsonAudreyBartRachelHarrietJacob
BobekCharlieHattieMichaelMalcolmBjornWesley
CurtisPenelopeBrittanyNatashaMorganAung
EmmanuelChristopherLonniePaulOlgaAngela
JoeyLornaLouis . . .

He wonders which of them was The Kid.

He takes the walnut half shell from his pocket. He's
tempted to listen to it once more, for old times' sake,
but he knows there is no longer anything to hear. The
Story has been told. He deposits the shell in the round
hole, and out of the slit with a cheerful *ching!* pops a
ticket. It does not say where he is going. It says simply:

ONE WAY

He does not breathe air inside the station—he
breathes names. They pass through him as if he is nothing. They race along his vessels, leap pumping from his
heart. He stands at the door. He clears his throat, for he

wants to say it right. He stands tall, for everything he has ever been, everything he is, and he joins them, boldly, proudly, better than he has ever said it, for it must last now and forever:

"Jack!"

He steps outside, closes the door.

It is dark.

He hears the whistle. It is getting louder.

He crosses the creek, makes his way through the trees to the tracks. They shine now, silver ribbons in the moonlight—and suddenly he has a thought. Something he wants to do. But the train is coming, faster now and faster. The train that never was now suddenly is—*is*—and he knows it will not wait for long.

He bolts across the tracks and scrambles up the impossible bluffside and races to the blackberry bramble. The junker bike is still there. He mounts it, races across the moonlit shadows to Gorilla Hill, plunges up it with every Jack he's ever been. The pedals become his legs, the wheels his lungs. He doesn't stop till he becomes the first ever to pedal-mount the peak. At night! He kickstands the nag, smacks it on the rump, whispers sternly in its ear. The moon is directly above him, the stars, the constellations twinkle across the sky, so many, one for every kid on Hokey Pokey and more. He has never seen such wondrous things.

Below him Hokey Pokey sleeps.

Campfires! he thinks. Then realizes he's looking down on a night-world of sleep monsters. From here, they might be the glowing embers of fallen stars.

Down there Dusty sleeps under the great pointing arm of The Kid. LaJo wherever. Somewhere Jubilee dreams beside her little brother. Kiki. Lopez. Harold the not-so-mighty Destroyer of Worlds. In the other direction a few stragglers stagger toward the trees, kids who can't sleep unless they cross the tracks, even the creek. Wanda is down there somewhere, Wanda and her dopey doughball of a monster. Beyond the Mountains the thunder seems to be cracking, breaking into . . . what? . . . babble? . . . voices? . . .

He stands on the bike seat. It wobbles but holds. He wishes he had thought to bring a stick, but maybe that's OK. He's about to find out if it's as close as he's always thought. The bike is no Scramjet; it's too unsteady. One good jump will have to do it. He crouches. He gathers himself. He pushes off, up to the sky, reaches, reaches for the moon, swats and—yes!—brushes it with his fingertips, catches just enough of it to set it trembling in the sky as the nag goes crashing. He falls to the ground. Flat on his back he sees the moon teeter above him. It sways. It circles like a bug going down a drain. It lurches drunkenly, and suddenly, with an audible *floop!* the moon pops from the sky and falls to the ground beside him. It bounces. He stops it from rolling down the hill. He sits up. He holds it in his lap. It's just as he has long suspected. It's about the size and color and feel of a soccer ball.

The train whistle is now a scream, a scream smothered by the monstrous chuff of the oncoming locomotive. A shaft of engine light skates off the track bend. *Time!* He leaps to his feet. He holds the moon in both hands. He punts it as high as he can. It bounces off constellations like a pinball and finally comes to rest where it had started, a bike-seat leap above his head.

Jack cups his hands to his mouth and sends one final Tarzan yell to his sleeping Amigos. The train is roaring. The light shaft is rocking up the tracks. He grabs the nag, flies down the hill.

LAJO

FOR A CHANGE, LaJo and Dusty are bunking together under The Kid's arm. LaJo dreams Jack is calling. Now the three of them are yipping and chasing the herd across the Plains and LaJo is about to lasso a black-and-gold beauty when he feels somebody pulling his finger and calling his name.

He opens his eyes. It's William the runt.

"LaJo! I finded you!"

LaJo recloses his eyes. "I'm sleeping."

Now the runt is pulling on LaJo's wrist with both hands. He's actually grunting with the effort. "C'mon, LaJo—let's play."

The Newbie's first day is over. LaJo's job is done. He doesn't ever have to see this kid again. So why is he staggering to his feet, allowing the sleepless runt to drag him off to who knows where? To Playground, it turns out, lit along the way by the soft glow of sleepers' monsters.

"Push me, LaJo!" the runt pipes, plopping onto a swing seat. LaJo pushes. The runt goes, "Wheeee!" Then it's on to the sliding board. The seesaw. The monkey bars. "Wheeee! Wheeee!"

"Cartoons!" cries the runt. He makes LaJo sit through *Scooby-Doo, The Flintstones* and, most painfully, Donald Duck's rich uncle, Scrooge McDuck. LaJo is fast asleep when he feels the finger-pull again. "LaJo! Hippodrome!"

They're riding a hippo mouth in a circle for about the hundredth time when LaJo finally catches a break. The runt is slumped against him, dead asleep. He eases himself away, steps off the carousel, walks—and stops. Stops and just stands there in the dark for no good reason. Turns for no good reason. Goes back to Hippodrome, grabs the runt, slings him over his shoulder and returns to The Kid for no good reason. Dusty is giggling in his sleep. LaJo lays the runt down, lays himself down.

The runt is between him and Dusty. The runt turns and flops his arm across LaJo's chest. LaJo is about to remove it. But doesn't. No good reason.

Now he's wide-awake. He crosses his hands under his head. Except for the runt's flopped arm, he wouldn't know there was anything but himself and the night. The sky. The stars. So many. He's never seen so many of anything. He lifts his head. There's the moon. Over Gorilla Hill as usual. It looks so low. Reminds him of a soccer ball. He knows it's crazy, but he can't help thinking that if he went over there right now, climbed up the hill and stood right under the moon, he could jump up and touch it.

TRAIN

THE TRAIN IS THERE, belching smoke, barely still. As Jack looks down from the rim of the bluff, a thin shower of grit falls on him. Steam gasps from the great iron wheels. He can feel the heat. Behind the engine is a parade of passenger cars. Their dull red color matches that of the bluff he stands on. They go on and on around the bend to the east. He wonders if there's a caboose.

Out of the first car steps the conductor, stubble-chinned but spiffy in black suit and brimmed cap. "All aboard!" he calls, looking up and down the tracks as if he doesn't know Jack stands above him. Jack skids down the bluffside, rushes to the train. "Almost didn't make it, kid," says the conductor. He moves aside so Jack can mount the steps.

Jack stands at the head of a long aisle of empty seats. He wonders if he's the only passenger. Above him a dim light flickers behind frosted glass. He chooses a seat on the right side. Then changes to the left. A window seat.

A flurry of chuffs: the train begins to move. The conductor comes down the aisle barking, "Tickets!" Jack hands over his ticket. The conductor punches it, but instead of handing it back, he keeps it. He pulls a round brass watch from his vest pocket. "Running late," he says, and moves on. For a moment Jack wants to call after him, wants to say *Where are we going?* But he doesn't.

As the train slowly gathers speed, he watches the bluff go by, then Gorilla Hill and Great Plains, milky in the moonlight, then nothing but trees. Panic rises. He glances back for the conductor but he is gone. He stands. "Stop! Wait!" He tries to open the window. It won't budge. He runs down the aisle to the next car, which is empty, and the next car, which is empty. Where is the conductor? He calls: "Stop the train! I want to get off! Please!" The ceiling lights flicker a final time and go out. The pale light of the moon skims the crests of a hundred empty seats. From the engine's heart beats a strong and steady rhythm.

Groping in the dark, he returns to his seat. For some reason it feels important to reclaim the same seat he started with. Occasionally a passing branch scratches at the window. He has to look back now to see the moon. He cannot find Gorilla Hill.

Why is this happening? Why must he go? He thinks he hears the Amigos calling him from the bluff. In the black glaze of the window he sees the faces of Hokey Pokey. Kids. Kids. From the other side of the window Jubilee smiles at him. Scramjet rears up majestically on his hind wheel. The herd thunders across Great Plains. Kiki pounds his fist into his glove, calls, "C'mon, Jack—send me a hard one!" He has been happy here. Happy. The Hokey Pokey Man flips his towel over the block of ice. The Hokey Pokey Man says, *Sayonara, kid.*

The train labors up a slope, now cruises onto flatlands, bogs of moongleaming pondwater and the contorted stumps of trees. It is so different here. Jack has never known anything but Hokey Pokey, has never known there was anything *but* Hokey Pokey. The train clatters over a bridge. His creek, where he explored and stone-crossed and poked at crayfish all his life, is but a trickle to the broad river below. The engine hurls its whistle into the night.

Jack looks back out the window and panics—the moon is not there! He rushes to the other side of the train—there it is, high above the bogs. When he returns to his seat, he sees dark, massive shapes receding in the distance. The Mountains. They have now passed beyond the Mountains that speak in thunder, the end of the world.

The bogs give way to a landscape of humpy hills, like dumped potatoes. Dinging, flashing red lights race by the window. He glimpses roads running into the tracks. He sees a light in the distance. A fallen star? Pale lights drizzle from unseen sources. The train rolls on.

Boxy shapes race by. In the distance a cluster of lights, some of them moving. Into the dark well of a tunnel and out to a hailstorm of lights on all sides. The train seems to be moving faster, seems excited. Jack's heart matches the pulsebeat of the screaming locomotive. The smell of burning coal fills the swaying, clattering car. He is thrilled. He is terrified. He wants to cry. He wants to cheer. There are no faces at the window now, only lights against the blackness. He closes his eyes. He breathes deeply . . . deeply . . . he is feeling creamy . . . he tries to remember . . .

NOT HOKEY POKEY

TOMORROW

JACK

"WAKE UP, Jack!"

He opens his eyes. A pelican is staring at him. A pelican with a bunch of mop-haired little kids peering wide-eyed over the lip of its basketball-size mouth pouch. The same wallpaper pelican he's been waking up to all his life.

The door opens. "Time's flyin, Mr. Boy. You're the one who wanted to do this." His father.

Do what?

He thinks. But he's sleepy. He thinks harder. He remembers. It's Saturday. The day his dad agreed to help him change his room. Get rid of those dumb pelicans once and for all. Strip off the wallpaper. Paint the walls. Some cool color. Black maybe. Or silver.

He gropes out of bed, staggers down the hallway to the bathroom, pees, splashes water on his face. Suddenly his mother is screaming: "Omygod!" He steps into the hallway. She's standing at the doorway to his room. She's leaning in, sniffing. Now she steps into the room, out of his sight. She's there for about a minute. Now he hears it again, slower this time: "Oh. My. God."

She reappears at his doorway. She's staring at him like he's a total stranger.

What did he do now? It's too early in the day to defend himself. Whatever it is, he'll confess.

Now she's coming his way. The look on her face, he's never seen it before. She stops in front of him. It occurs to him that her eyes are on the same level as his. Yes! He's no longer shorter than his mother. He tries to find *mad* in the look she's giving him. He can't.

Her look is changing again. Now it's puzzled. "Jack," she says, and now he thinks she's actually looking *up* at him a little. "Jack," she repeats, like she wants to be sure she got his name right, "has anyone else been in your room? I mean, like, since yesterday?"

He wonders if parents begin to go dotty in their early forties. "No," he says. He kind of wants to ask *Why?* but he really doesn't want to get into a conversation.

"You're sure?"

He gives her a glare that says: *I'm not gonna take this anymore. Now will you please step aside so I can get back to my room.*

She reads his glare. She has always read his glares perfectly, way better than Dad. But she doesn't step aside. She takes his shoulders in her hands. The look on her face is becoming half smile, half wonder. "One more question."

"Mom," he says, "one more question and I'm gonna have to shove you outta the way."

She knows he's joking. She leans into him until the top of her head is resting against his chin. He can smell her shampoo. Like April. He wants to squirm away but dares not. She chuckles softly. He hears her breathe words into his shirt, but they make no sense.

"Huh?" he says.

She backs off, repeats herself into his eyes. "I can't find your dirty socks anywhere. They're not under the bed or in the closet. Where are they?"

"I ate them," he says.

"Where *are* they?" She's smiling and she's wonder-eyed but there's something else too. Bulldog. She won't let it go.

"In the hamper," he says.

Her breath catches. For a moment he thinks she's going to cry. He'd never have guessed she could squeeze his shoulders this hard. "And who"—she's having trouble saying it—"*who* put them in the hamper?"

"Me" is barely out of his mouth before she's hugging him and rocking him from wall to wall and laughing her head off and calling, "Richard—wait till you hear this!" She holds him at arm's length, looks him up and down, shakes her head. "Never thought I'd see the day." She crashes into him again, kisses him and is gone, dancing down the hallway—a quick look into the bathroom ("And he turned off the water!"), dancing down the stairway, pumping her arms like a cheerleader. "My baby is growing up!"

Whatever. He reminds himself that his mother does acting at the Hedgerow Playhouse. When he calls her *hysterical*, she says *theatrical*. Safely back in his room, he mightily wants to flop into bed but doesn't. He gets dressed. He grabs a felt-tip poster marker and does what he's wanted to do for a long time—he scribbles all over the stupid pelicans.

Proof that he did something good is waiting for him at the breakfast table: blueberry pancakes. His all-time favorite. His mother keeps turning from the stove, saying, "More?" He's relieved to see she's no longer going nutso. He keeps catching her staring at him. He's on his last bite when his father comes in. "Let's move, pal. Places to go. We're already late. Anything not done today you'll have to finish on your own." Thankfully, his male parent is his usual crisp, all-business self.

As they head for the front door, his father glances into the den, says, "Kiki, back off." His little brother is there, as always on a Saturday, cross-legged on the rug, his face about three millimeters from the TV screen, watching his cartoons. As his brother pushes himself backward on the rug, Jack sees he's been sitting on Mr. Shortstop. Kiki senses Jack, turns, waves the glove. "Play catch, Jack?"

"Later," says Jack. "Gotta get some paint with Dad."

Kiki re-sits himself on the glove, turns back to the screen. Jack hears, "Ehh . . . what's up, Doc?" Bugs Bunny. Kiki's favorite.

Before his father can open the door, there's a knock. It's the little Lopez girl—Gracie—barefoot and wide-eyed, from up the street. "Can Kiki come out to play?"

"If you can tear him away from his cartoons," says his father. He steps aside. "Go ahead and try." The girl runs past Jack, calling, "Kiki! Kiki! Let's go to the playground!" She's trying to yank him away from the screen. Good luck.

His father wags his head. "Kids," he says, chuckling. "They live in their own little world."

Outside, the sun is dazzling. He hears a couple of lawn mowers going already. There are kids up and down the street, mostly little. Any respectable teenager is still in bed. Across the street, little kids are killing each other with everything from lightsabers to golden pistols. There's a black-taped ball in the driveway, smeary with yellow dust. He kicks it aside.

As they head for the car, his attention is caught by a bike moving down the sidewalk across the street. It's the girl from the next block. Jubilee Trimble. Hair flying behind her baseball cap. As she goes by, she seems to look in his direction. He smiles at memories of their little kidhoods, when they tormented each other daily as sworn enemies. It occurs to him to wave to her, but by the time he decides this, she's halfway down the block.

In the car his father is saying something about paint and wallpaper stripping, but Jack is noticing something in the pocket of his jeans, something that wasn't there before. He takes it out. It's a yellow ribbon. His first impulse is to throw it away, but he does not. The ribbon is fat and bold. Such a ribbon might wrap a spectacular gift. Where did it come from? Why does he have it? He runs his finger over it. As the engine comes to life and they back down the driveway, he turns away so his father cannot see. He sniffs the yellow ribbon. *Girl.* He touches it to his lips.

He opens his window, catches the breeze. As they cruise through the neighborhood, he hears, from somewhere behind them, a kid's voice. Shouting. Yodeling. Sounds like a Tarzan yell.

HOKEY POKEY

NIGHT

Lɪᴏɴ ʏᴀᴡɴs and inhales six of the Seven Sisters, who then come laughing out of his nostrils. "Do it again!" they plead, but Lion roars and that's the signal for the party to start. Bulls. Bears. Dippers. Swans. Archers. Queens. Kings. Rams. Maidens. Crabs. Twins. Flying fish. Sea goats. From all quarters of the heavens they come and make a circle a million stars around and do the hokey pokey . . .

Put your right paw out . . .

. . . till the sky itself wobbles with laughter, and no one notices Pitcher Boy, for he is very still. Little Bear stubs his toe on a leftover wish and howls so loud he awakens Mooncow, who glumpers to the top of the sky and pours a Milky Way, and now the dancing circle is a wild white flume ride across the endless night. And Pitcher Boy might have stayed still till dawn, but Little Bear howls on and Pitcher Boy dips his pitcher into Milky Way and pours it over Little Bear, who gubbles and gurps and burps a milky bubble, a magnificent bubble that sails among the chuckling stars and becomes pearly with starlight, heavy with starlight, and falls . . . falls down . . .

down . . .

down . . .

down . . .

TODAY

JUBILEE

. . . TO HOKEY POKEY . . .

   . . . where it breaks with a soft and golden *pip!* upon the nose of Jubilee, breaks and spills over her sleeping eyes a whispered word:

it's

and then another:

time

ACKNOWLEDGMENTS

Many thanks to my associate storytellers:

Roger Adelman

Rinky Batson

Shorty Landes

Renée Cafiero

Nancy Hinkel

Bill Reiss

Eileen

Read an excerpt from
MILKWEED
by JERRY SPINELLI

1

MEMORY

I am running.

That's the first thing I remember. Running. I carry some-thing, my arm curled around it, hugging it to my chest. Bread, of course. Someone is chasing me. "Stop! Thief!" I run. People. Shoulders. Shoes. "Stop! Thief!"

Sometimes it is a dream. Sometimes it is a memory in the middle of the day as I stir iced tea or wait for soup to heat. I never see who is chasing and calling me. I never stop long enough to eat the bread. When I awaken from dream or mem-ory, my legs are tingling.

2

SUMMER

He was dragging me, running. He was much bigger. My feet skimmed over the ground. Sirens were screaming. His hair was red. We flew through streets and alleyways. There were thumping noises, like distant thunder. The people we bounced off didn't seem to notice us. The sirens were screaming like babies. At last we plunged into a dark hole.

"You're lucky," he said. "Soon it won't be ladies chasing you. It will be Jackboots."

"Jackboots?" I said.

"You'll see."

I wondered who the Jackboots were. Were unfooted boots running along the streets?

"Okay," he said, "hand it over."

"Hand what over?" I said.

He reached into my shirt and pulled out the loaf of bread. He broke it in half. He shoved one half at me and began to eat the other.

"You're lucky I didn't kill you," he said. "That lady you took this from, I was just getting ready to snatch it for myself."

"I'm lucky," I said.

He burped. "You're quick. You took it before I even knew

what happened. That lady was rich. Did you see the way she was dressed? She'll just buy ten more."

I ate my bread.

More thumping sounds in the distance. "What is that?" I asked him.

"Jackboot artillery," he said.

"What's artillery?"

"Big guns. Boom boom. They're shelling the city." He stared at me. "Who are you?"

I didn't understand the question.

"I'm Uri," he said. "What's your name?"

I gave him my name. "Stopthief."

3

He took me to meet the others. We were in a stable. The horses were there. Usually they would be out on the streets, but they were home now because the Jackboots were boom-booming the city and it was too dangerous for horses. We sat in a stall near the legs of a sad-faced gray. The horse pooped. Two of the kids got up and went to the next stall, another horse. A moment later came the sound of water splashing on straw. The two came back. One of them said, "I'll take the poop."

"Where did you find him?" said a boy smoking a cigarette.

"Down by the river," said Uri. "He snatched a loaf from a rich lady coming out of the Bread Box."

Another boy said, "Why didn't you snatch it from him?" This one was smoking a cigar as long as his face.

Uri looked at me. "I don't know."

"He's a runt," someone said. "Look at him."

"Stand up," said someone else.

I looked at Uri. Uri flicked his finger. I stood.

"Go there," someone said. I felt a foot on my back, pushing me toward the horse.

"See," said the cigar smoker, "he doesn't even come halfway up to the horse's dumper."

A voice behind me squawked, "The horse could dump a new hat on him!"

Everyone, even Uri, howled with laughter. Explosions went off beyond the walls.

The boys who were not smoking were eating. In the corner of the stable was a pile as tall as me. There was bread in all shapes and sausages of all lengths and colors and fruits and candies. But only half of it was food. All sorts of other things glittered in the pile. I saw watches and combs and ladies' lipsticks and eyeglasses. I saw the thin flat face of a fox peering out.

"What's his name?" said someone.

Uri nodded at me. "Tell them your name."

"Stopthief," I said.

Someone crowed, "It speaks!"

Smoke burst from mouths as the boys laughed.

One boy did not laugh. He carried a cigarette behind each ear. "I think he's cuckoo."

Another boy got up and came over to me. He leaned down. He sniffed. He pinched his nose. "He smells." He blew smoke into my face.

"Look," someone called, "even the smoke can't stand him. It's turning green!"

They laughed.

The smoke blower backed off. "So, Stopthief, are you a smelly cuckoo?"

I didn't know what to say.

"He's stupid," said the unlaughing boy. "He'll get us in trouble."

"He's quick," said Uri. "And he's little."

"He's a runt."

"Runt is good," said Uri.

"Are you a Jew?" said the boy in my face.

"I don't know," I said.

He kicked my foot. "How can you not know? You're a Jew or you're not a Jew."

I shrugged.

"I told you, he's stupid," said the unlaugher.

"He's young," said Uri. "He's just a little kid."

"How old are you?" said the smoke blower.

"I don't know," I said.

The smoke blower threw up his hands. "Don't you know *anything*?"

"He's stupid."

"He's a stupid Jew."

"A *smelly* stupid Jew."

"A *tiny* smelly stupid Jew!"

More laughter. Each time they laughed, they threw food at each other and at the horse.

The smoke blower pressed my nose with the tip of his finger. "Can you do this?" He leaned back until he was facing the ceiling. He puffed on the cigarette until his cheeks, even his eyes, were bulging. His face looked like a balloon. It was grinning. I was sure he was going to destroy me with his faceful of smoke, but he didn't. He turned to the horse, lifted its tail, and blew a stream of silvery smoke at the horse's behind. The horse nickered.

Everyone howled. Even the unlaugher. Even me.

The pounding in the distance was like my heartbeat after running.

"He must be a Jew," someone said.

"What's a Jew?" I said.

"Answer the runt," someone said. "Tell him what a Jew is."

The unlaugher kicked ground straw at a boy who hadn't spoken. The boy had only one arm. "That's a Jew." He pointed to himself. "This is a Jew." He pointed to the others. "That's a Jew. That's a Jew. That's a Jew." He pointed to the horse. "That's a Jew." He fell to his knees and scrabbled in the straw near the horse flop. He found something. He held it out to me. It was a small brown insect. "This is a Jew. Look. *Look!*" He startled me. "A Jew is an animal. A Jew is a bug. A Jew is less than a bug." He threw the insect into the flop. "A Jew is *that*."

Others cheered and clapped.

"Yeah! Yeah!"

"I'm a horse turd!"

"I'm a goose turd!"

A boy pointed at me. "He's a Jew all right. Look at him. He's a Jew if I ever saw one."

"Yeah, he's in for it all right."

I looked at the boy who spoke. He was munching on a sausage. "What am I in for?" I said.

He snorted. "Strawberry babka."

"We're all in for it," said someone else. "We're in for it good."

"Speak for yourself," said the unlaugher. He came and stood before me. He reached down and fingered the yellow stone hung around my neck on a string. "What's this?" he said.

"I don't know," I said.

"Where did you get it?"

"I always had it."

He let go of the stone. He backed off to arm's length. He wet his finger with spit and rubbed my cheek. "He's a Gypsy."

There were gasps of wonder. The others leaned forward, munching, puffing their tobaccos.

"How do you know?"

"Look at his eyes. How black. And his skin. And this." He flicked the yellow stone.

The smoke blower said, "You're a Gypsy, ain't you?"

It sounded familiar. I had heard that word before, around me, in a room, near a wagon.

I nodded.

"Get him out of here," said the sausage muncher. "We don't need Gypsies. They're dirt."

The smoke blower laughed. "Look who's talking."

The one-armed boy spoke for the first time. "Next to Jews, they hate Gypsies the most."

"There's a difference," said another. "Everybody doesn't hate the Gypsies, but there's nobody that doesn't hate us. Nobody is hated close to us. They even hate us in Washington America."

"Because we boil babies and eat them for matzoh!" someone growled scarily.

Everyone laughed and threw food.

"We drink people's blood!"

"We suck their brains out through their noses with a straw!"

"Even *cannibals* hate us!"

"Even *monkeys* hate us!"

"Even *cockroaches* hate us!"

Words and laughter and bread and sausages flew through the

tobacco smoke and the horse's legs. Hands reached for the pile. Golden bracelets flew and jars of jam and tiny painted animals and fountain pens. The flanks of the horse flickered as they were pelted. A white-and-purple glass fish bounced off my forehead. The fox fur flew. One boy paraded wearing it about his shoulders, kissing its snout.

And then the stableman was coming and shouting and we were running, and outside we scattered like cockroaches and I ran with Uri and the thumping explosions were louder and the clouds in the sky were brown and black.

We ran through streets and alleyways to the back of a small brick building. Uri threw open a wooden hatch, and we plunged into a dark, cool cellar. Uri pulled down the hatch, snipping off the daylight, then he flipped a switch and a bare lightbulb burned among the cobwebs in the ceiling.

Uri pointed upward. "It's a barbershop. The barber went. He left everything. I'll show you tomorrow."

The cellar was a home. Carpets covered the floor. There was a bed and a chair and a radio and a chest of drawers. Even an icebox.

"Tonight you sleep on the floor," he said. "Tomorrow I'll get you a bed."

The explosions stopped, or maybe I just couldn't hear them anymore. We ate bread and jam and slices of salty meat.

I said, "What am I in for?"

He did not look at me. "You heard. Strawberry babka. Eat."

4

When I awoke the next morning, Uri was gone. He returned dragging a mattress. It was small, about half the size of his, but plenty big enough for me.

I lay down on it. He jerked me to my feet and snapped, "Not yet." He hauled me outside.

We walked to the shopping district, where the big stores were. Except some of them were not so big now; the bombardment had left them crumples of brick. Looking down the street, I saw spaces where stores should be. Like broken teeth.

We went behind the stores, to alleyways of trucks and trash bins and staring cats. Uri said, "Wait here." He disappeared in a maze of air shafts and fire escapes and doors, and when he came out his arms were loaded with clothes. "For you," he said.

I reached.

"Don't touch. Follow me."

He led me to a bombed-out building, nothing but the back wall standing. We climbed over a jumble of bricks and splintered wood and twisted pipe. "Watch the glass," he said. I kept stumbling over the heads and arms of manikins. We came to a lopped-off stairway. Uri tested it. "Okay," he said. We went down into the rubble. Whenever he came to a knob in a pipe, he turned it. Some gave out steam, some nothing. We stopped at one that gave water.

"Take those rags off," he said. I took off my clothes. He laid down the new ones and went rooting through the rubble. He returned with a manikin's leg and a scrub brush. He filled the leg with water. "I'm not thirsty," I said. He dumped the water over me. He began to scrub me with the brush.

At first it felt wonderful. Then it didn't. Leg after leg of water he poured over me. After the scrub brush got down to the soles of my feet, he started again on my face. He grunted as he scrubbed. I squirmed. I cried out. He was scrubbing my skin off.

At last he stopped. "Baby," he said. He dried me with a shirt. I screamed in pain from the rubbing. He patted the rest of me dry.

He glared at me. "Did you *ever* have a bath?" I stared at him. "Didn't think so."

Then he dressed me in a clean shirt and too-big pants. People gave us looks as we climbed out of the rubble and onto the sidewalk. By the time we were halfway home, I was feeling terrific. I felt new. I felt the air, the sun on my skin. Uri brought his nose to my neck and sniffed. He nodded.

Back in the cellar we ate sugar cookies and jars of plums in syrup. Then he led me upstairs to the barbershop. I had never been in a barbershop. He was right: the barber had left every-thing. Rows of colored liquid—green, red, blue—lined the shelf beneath a great mirror.

"You never had your hair cut, did you?" he said.

"No," I said.

"Have a seat."

I climbed into the red padded chair. He spun me around till I got dizzy. He pumped a lever and I rose higher. He shook out a large cloth and draped it over me. From a glass canister he

pulled a comb and scissors and he began combing and snipping. Soon my hair was like fur.

"All right," he said, "which one?"

"Which one?" I echoed.

He pointed to the bottles. I did not understand why I should
be offered a drink after having my hair cut, but I didn't argue.
I had learned never to turn down food.

I pointed to the blue. "That one."

To my surprise he did not give me a drink but instead poured
the blue liquid over my head. He shuffled his fingers through
my hair and then combed it. It became wet and shiny.

Outside, people hurried this way and that. Many carried
shovels.

"Are they going to a farm?" I said.

"They're digging trenches to stop the tanks," he said.

"What's a tank?"

"You'll see."

Soldiers marched and ran and blew whistles. People carried
large fat bags. They must have been heavy, for one person
could carry only one at a time, over his shoulders. If you had a
wheelbarrow, you could take three.

"What's in the bags?" I said.

"Sand," he said.

I found out where the bags of sand went. I saw them stacked
in front of machine guns in doorways and on roofs and at the
ends of streets.

We hopped a streetcar as it rattled down the tracks. We got
footholds on the outside and clung to window posts. The wind

blew through my new hair. Passengers frowned at us. "Get off," they said.

"Look," said Uri.

A boy was running along the sidewalk at the same speed as us. It was the boy who blew smoke in my face. His arms were wrapped around a lamp of pure white glass in the shape of a naked woman. The lampshade fell off, but he kept running, weaving in and out of sidewalk people. I looked behind him. A man was chasing him, shouting, "Stop him!"

Uri swung out from the side of the streetcar like a gate. He waved. "Hey, Kuba!"

Kuba looked over as he ran. "Hey, Uri!"

It was then that someone stuck out a foot and tripped him. Kuba went sprawling, and the pure white naked woman shattered on the sidewalk. "Get him!" someone yelled, and the sidewalk people converged on Kuba.

"They won't get him," Uri said.

As the streetcar rattled on down the tracks, I saw someone swing a leg out and kick, and then Kuba was popping from the crowd and racing across the street, and the people hurled curses and laughter after him.

Uri shook his head grimly. "Stupid. Stupid. They take everything. Just to take it." He looked at me as the streetcar clanged above us. "Take only what you need. You hear?" He pinched my nose until my eyes watered.

I howled. "Yes!"

For a minute the passengers had forgotten us as they stared at the excitement on the sidewalk. Now they remembered us. A man in a silver necktie snarled, "Go. Get off." A little boy stuck out his tongue. And then a woman in a fox fur came down the aisle and reached over the seats and drew down the window on Uri's hands. I screamed, but Uri didn't. The fox's eyes were like little black marbles. The lady reached over to bring down my window too, but she stopped because there was a loud sound, and it wasn't the clang of the streetcar. It was sirens. Ahead of us a shop exploded in a gush of flame.

People screamed. The streetcar gasped and jerked to a halt. Within moments it was empty. Even the driver was gone, running with the crowds in the street.

And then the streets were empty. A strange music filled the air: the sirens' wail and the thump of exploding shells.

I pulled myself up into the streetcar. I opened the window that clamped Uri's fingers. He fell to the ground and in a moment appeared at the door. He threw his hands in the air and cheered, "Finally!"

I thought he was celebrating the release of his fingers, but it was something else. "I always wanted to drive one of these." He sat in the driver's seat. He stared at the controls. He pushed one thing, pulled another; the streetcar jerked into movement and we were heading down the tracks.

What a ride! Uri turned the steering stick this way and that. He learned how to make it go faster, then faster, and the street-car screamed along with us through the deserted city. Smoke rose beyond the rooftops, as if giants were puffing cigars. He showed me where to pull the clanger, and I pulled and pulled and the clanging joined the music of the bombardment.

At last we came to a loop, where the streetcar was meant to turn around, but Uri did not slow down, and the streetcar leaped from the tracks, and it was like riding a house into other houses. We smashed into a restaurant, plowed through a field of red tablecloths into the kitchen with an ear-ripping clatter, and still there were no people and no one to yell, "Stop! Stop!" Sauerkraut splattered across the windshield as we came to a halt against the ovens. By now the streetcar was on its side and we were hanging from our places. Uri was howling like a wolf, and even as the oven chimney pipes toppled like trees, I laughed and pulled and pulled the clanger rope.